SAVAGE KING

THE CRYSTAL KINGDOM: NEW WORLDS

MILLY TAIDEN

SAVAGE KING

THE CRYSTAL KINGDOM: NEW WORLDS

NEW YORK TIMES and USA TODAY
BESTSELLING AUTHOR
MILLY TAIDEN

ABOUT THE BOOK

Through magic gone totally wrong, Wren and her cousins wind up on Gecire, sister dimension to the Crystal Kingdom.

Wren McClure, journalist by day, romance writer by night, has a hard time facing the world's ever-increasing responsibilities. Her life is already pretty messy. She doesn't have time to think of falling in love, but she has no say in matters of her heart. Not when a big, sexy shifter decides she's his.

Xenos Woodsky, alpha of the Gnoleon fae, has endured over three hundred years of self-induced solitude for a mistake that killed many in his tribe.

When his mate portals into his reclusive life, he's forced into taking action. It's time to return to his people. It's time to claim the woman he wants.

Old enemies come back and the tribe is forced to move. They need everyone's help, especially Xenos. Xenos has to decide if he's going to face up for past actions with his people and save the day, or lose his mate and his tribe.

Published By
Latin Goddess Press
Winter Springs, FL 32708
http://millytaiden.com
Savage King
Copyright © 2020 by Milly Taiden
Edited by: Tina Winograd
Cover: Jacqueline Sweet

❀ Created with Vellum

—For My Readers

Thank you for loving the Crystal Kingdom!

I hope you love Xenos and Wren's book. I hope you stay with me in the journey into the Crystal Kingdom: New Worlds

PROLOGUE

He smelled his prey's fear. The air was heavy, the scent sticking to giant leaves in his hot, humid home. The kappy raced to get away, but his meal was too fun not to catch. He wanted to chuckle, but creatures like him couldn't do that. Instead he chuffed. If he had remembered the words, he would've taunted the kappy. After all, cats did like to play with their food.

At an easy lope, he followed the trail through the jungle. His meal had a long way to go before it reached its home in the caves. Plus, with only two legs, it was slow. His four paws making no sound, he ducked under large leaves from the overwhelming flora covering the ground. Most going higher than a fae stood.

Bugs and small animals scampered out of his way. They recognized when a predator was near. Birds in the dense foliage overhead quieted after squealing a warning to anything around that could hear them. Normally he cursed the flying bastards, but this hunt didn't depend on stealth. It was about who could go on the longest. And he could go on a damnation long time.

An orange flower launched its poisonous dart at him, his thick fur and hide barely moved when it hit and bounced off. Stupid plants. If they tasted good, he would've chewed on them. A memory from his past tried to wiggle free from the hole he'd buried them in long ago. Never. He stopped that dragon shit before it even started.

His senses alerted him that something was going to happen. Then not too far in the distance, an explosion shook the ground. Sounded like trees snapping in half. What the hell?

He had a choice: continue after his morning meal or check out what happened in his territory. His stomach twisted, making the decision for him. Thank the goddess. Picking up speed, he was tiring of the chase. He was hungry and wanted to get this over with.

Then his senses gave him the same warning, and another explosion rattled the ground much closer.

He focused his eyes as he padded along, peering through the dense vegetation for anything unusual. The air crackled with a strange smell, like something burning. The trees ahead were bent and broken. He stepped into a round patch of sunlight that had never reached this dirt before.

In almost a perfect circle, the area was cleared of all greenery, stripped of ground covering and top layer of dirt. What the goddess's hell?

He noticed movement on the other side of the circle. His prey had stopped too, its eyes wide and mouth hanging open. The expression was familiar, but he couldn't remember what it meant.

His body tingled a third time, much stronger than earlier. It was a warning of imminent danger. He spun around to run, then his ass end lifted high into the air and he flipped several times before he crashed upside down against a leaning tree, sliding toward the ground, and stopping when his head touched dirt.

In front of him in the clearing, a circle floated a

short distance off the ground. Inside that ring stood three females dressed in strange clothing. The space around them wasn't jungle, but forest and grassland. How was that possible?

As he watched, the trio stepped out of the other place and into his. Then they tumbled to the ground like newborn cubs learning to walk.

What in demon's hell had just invaded his planet?

CHAPTER ONE

"**I**t's about damn time, girl."

Resting under one of the tree houses in the new dragon/dark elf forest home, Wren lifted her brow at Daphne's comment. Usually, the woman never had a negative thing to say, even when everyone knew she was angry. She always bottled it up and looked the other way. One of these days that would bite her in the ass.

But Wren supposed it was better than what she did herself, which was freak out in a panic attack, then hide herself for days writing stories she had control over. Where she could make the world how she wanted it.

From where Daphne sat against a tree in the new village of Elgon in the Crystal Kingdom, she climbed to her feet and brushed off the back of her jean shorts.

"Hey, shut it," Lilah snapped. "Next time, you go find Chelsea in the fucking food fields. I had to go all the way to the other side of this place." Lilah threw Grandmom's magic stone at Daphne. The girl lifted her hands to shield herself and ducked. Not that Lilah had good enough aim to tag her. The rock flew past at least a foot away, bouncing on the ground.

Wren shook her head. Those two fought like sisters instead of cousins. "Lilah," she said, "be careful with that. They aren't normal stones. You might break it."

Standing in front of Wren, Lilah slapped a hand on her plump hip. "Break a magic rock? Yeah, right."

"You don't know," Daphne huffed, joining them after reclaiming the stone.

"Neither do you." Lilah said to Daphne, then spun on her heel. "Let's get this portal open. I have to work tomorrow."

Wren saw the expression on Daphne's face. If looks could kill. . .But it had always been that way. Lilah being bossy, and Daphne keeping it inside her.

She put her hand on Daphne's arm. "Why don't you say something to her," Wren asked. "She's bossy, and she knows it."

Her cousin shook her head, stepping forward. "It won't do any good. When she's in a mood, there's no changing it."

Wren knew that all too well, but she'd stood up to her grumpy cousin when they were young girls. Since then, Lilah seldom pulled that kind of shit on her. She wished Daphne would have the courage to do the same. But what could she do? Daph had to do it herself.

She followed her cousins to the edge of a village. "Where are we going?" Wren asked.

"Chelsea said to keep this portal thing on the down low," Lilah answered.

"Why?"

Lilah shrugged. "I don't know. Something about the little elflings wanting to go to Earth."

Wren smiled. That would be chaos the planet wasn't prepared for. A dozen young elves running around, using magic to take every candy bar and sugar-filled drink they could find.

Actually, that was an interesting idea. Maybe she could work that into a plot line with a little suspense. Who could resist adorable little elves with big eyes and Spock ears? Of course, she'd have to work in the shifter tigers she was known for.

Well, maybe not totally "known for." As a daytime journalist, nighttime romance writer, nobody knew her from a hole in the wall. But one of these days. . .

Magical stone on her palm, Lilah held her hand out to her. "Here, take this one," Lilah said. Wren hesitated to take it. A bad feeling crept over her. How many stories had she written with the inciting incident being a stupid move on the main character's part? But in this story, she wondered who the lead female was.

"Maybe we should have Chelsea or Avery here," she said. "I mean, they are the ones with real experience with magic."

Lilah rolled her eyes. "Wren, stop worrying. We'll be fine. All we have to do is touch all three rocks together like Grandmom did, then, voila, we're home."

Daphne stared at the rock in her hand. "Grandmom said she would port over and get us. Maybe we should wait for her." Wren felt better knowing Daphne wasn't sure about this whole thing, either.

Lilah huffed. "Come on, guys. She won't be here for hours, and I'm tired of eating berries and nuts. I need some good shit, like potato chips and ice cream. Plus, I want a hot shower."

Both she and Daphne groaned in agreement. A tub of steaming water and lots of lavender soap sounded awesome. After the past days of helping the new residents of Elgon get settled into their new homes, she was ready to put her feet up and relax. What was supposed to be a surprise visit for Avery's birthday turned into a day with "Three Men and a Truck," minus the truck. And more than three hot men.

Damn, the entire village was made up of hot guys she'd spend years licking with delight. She had enough eye candy to write a decade's worth of romance books.

"All right," Daphne said, holding out her stone, "I so want a hot soak and to get out of these clothes. Yuck."

They definitely weren't dressed for manual labor. If Wren had known what they were going to do, she would've worn her sports bra and running shoes. What she had on barely held up her size-Ds anymore. It wasn't meant to be worn so long. Of course, with D boobs, no over-the-shoulder-boulder-holder would last very long.

She held out her rock. "I'm ready. How do we do this?"

"Grandmom touched all three rocks together, and the portal appeared." Lilah held her palm flat, stone on top. "Y'all put yours against mine."

"One at a time or together?"

Lilah scrunched her brows. She would have a cow if she knew how many wrinkles she was creating. It would age her faster than she wanted.

"Do one at a time."

Great. Her cousin was clueless. But now, Wren really wanted to wash her hair and watch the Bachelor. Tonight was the first rose ceremony.

Daphne placed her stone against Lilah's, then Wren touched hers to Lilah's. Next thing she knew, she was on her back staring at the cornflower blue sky, her ears ringing so loudly, she couldn't hear anything else. She rolled her head to the side to see her cousins in the same prone position. "What happened? Did we do something wrong?"

Lilah sat up, rubbing her head. "Maybe we should touch the stones together at the same time."

"You think?" Daphne hollered. "I'm flat on my ass—"

Lilah whipped her head around to Daph. "Hey—"

"Lilah," Wren warned, catching her attention. "Let's just try it again, okay?" What was wrong with her bitchy cousin? Lately, it seemed she was always in a bad mood and never wanted to go out anymore. She just sat at home all weekend. Something was up and she needed to find out what.

After sliding her foot in the slip-on sandal that flew off when the first portal's energy shoved them back, Wren gathered with the other two girls.

"On the count of three," Daphne said. "One, two. . ." They pressed their stones to each other creating another explosion, but this one they were ready for and remained standing. There in front of them floated the circle entrance to Earth. It was already night there as Wren could barely make out the trees in the darkness.

"Wait," Lilah said, "why isn't it Grandmom's living room? That's where we left."

Wren wanted to say "duh," but gave her cousin a break. "Because we're in a different place. If you want to go straight into her house, we have to go back to Avery's village where we came through. And I, for one, am not up for the hike."

"Not to mention that's rude," Daphne said.

"What if Grandmom and Grandpop were getting it on and we just appeared there?"

"They're eighty years old," she said. "You can't do that when you're eighty."

Daphne's brows rose on her head. "They have pills for that kind of thing."

"But eighty?"

Lilah sighed. "Let's go. I don't want to think about my grandmother getting more than I am."

Wren and Daphne laughed. "I know, right?" Daph said. They broke apart, and the portal disappeared.

"Well, shit," they said in three-piece harmony, then all laughed. Yeah, they were closer than cousins, tighter than sisters.

"Guess we have to cross keeping the stones together." Wren held her palm out.

"But we didn't have to with Grandmom?"

"I know, but Grandmom isn't here," Wren replied. "This time we move as a team, okay?"

Mumbled *yeah*s came from the others. Once again, they stood against the blast of air, the portal appearing. "Okay," Wren said, "baby steps scoot closer." They focused on keeping the rocks touching as they moved toward the opening to another dimension.

"I see trees," Lilah said. "You sure that's the woods behind Grandmom's."

"These are her stones, right?" Wren said, "Wouldn't it make sense they were tied to her property?"

"I'm not up on the rules of magic," Lilah replied. "I was out sick that day of school."

"You were not," Daphne said. "You had perfect attendance in school. My mom made it a point that I knew you were so much better than I was."

Lilah gave Wren a look, and they both laughed.

"What?" Daphne said. "What did I say that's so funny?" The girl's arm moved, almost taking her rock away.

"Watch it, Daph," Wren said. They were at the portal, and she felt the vibration it gave off in the air. Was that the magic or something else causing it? The heat and humidity blew through. "Okay, both of you step through together." Wren leaned forward with her arms out to move with them. When her cousins crossed over, she wasn't ready for them to pull her forward. Her flip-flop slipped from her foot again.

"Shit. Wait," she said, "my shoe."

"What do you mean your shoe—"

She bent down to secure it. "It's slipping—"

"Wren! You're moving your stone—"

"I just need to get my—"

"It'll close on you!"

A hand wrapped around her wrist, yanking her forward. Her shoe dangled off her big toe as she plunged headfirst into the other two with a short shriek. With an *oomph,* all three landed hard. The portal disappeared. Wren spit out the dirt in her mouth from lying face down.

"That was brilliant," Lilah said, sitting up. "I think I broke my ass."

"And that's a lot of ass to break," Wren replied, hiding a smile.

Lilah snorted. This was old banter between them. Lilah loved her hourglass shape, even though it was a large hourglass. "Better a big butt than no butt and all boob."

"I happen to like my flat butt. Men look at my face when introducing themselves, not at my ass."

"Wrong," Daphne added. "They can't take their eyes off your chest. Big boobs are a blessing."

Wren could argue with that, but now wasn't the time.

"Both of you stop complaining," Daphne rolled over. "Wren, you could've been cut in half if that portal would've closed on you. You know that, right?"

The thought slapped her in the face. Shit. Her cousin was right. What would've happened with part of her on one side and part on the other? Would she have been sliced in half? Blood spewing everywhere. How long would she have been in agony before finally dying? Who would water her plants at her home? Not to mention she was in the middle of a book with a tight deadline. She had to pay her bills. Her heart jumped in her chest, as fear clutched her stomach. Her throat dried. Beginnings of a panic attack.

Calm down, Wren. Deep breath. Still lying on her stomach, she clenched her hands into fists and hid them under her chin. Nobody knew how bad she'd gotten in the past six months. She was too embarrassed to ask for help. Her mom would blow it off, calling her a hypochondriac, while her father didn't care if she had problems at all.

Lilah held out a hand to help her up. She couldn't take it yet. "Wren?" Lilah said, worry in her voice.

Letting out a loud breath, she got control of herself, and she pushed onto her elbows. "Oh, thanks," she took the help, trying to play it off, "I didn't see your hand." She climbed to her feet, looking around the darkness. The sun had set or hadn't come up yet. She wasn't sure of the time difference between Earth and the Crystal Kingdom. She should've asked Grandmom more questions before coming on this visit to her cousin's.

When her eyes made out the giant jungle-like foliage outside the circle of dirt they stood in, bile climbed the back of her throat. This wasn't the woods around Grandmom's lake house.

From the hours she'd spent in the forest around the lake as a kid, she knew every tree and had climbed most of them. When the world became too much for her, with a romance book in hand, she'd disappear into the woods and sit in the limbs of the mighty elms and walnut trees. From there, she escaped into the world of shifters and their mates. Sometimes it was vampires and ghosts, but shifters were always her favorite.

It had been years since she'd been back there, but she knew this wasn't right. Her pulse picked up again.

She tightened her hand, feeling for a rock that was not there. "My stone," she said, hearing the tremor in her own voice. "Where's my stone?" She dropped to her knees, blindly reaching under fern fronds, her hands frantically slapping the moist ground. Her heart beat so hard, it hurt. Her lunch rose in her throat.

Lilah knelt beside her. "It's got to be here, Wren." A hand pressed on the back of her shoulder and squeezed. "We'll find it, okay?"

She nodded, breathing too hard to talk normally. This was her fault if they were lost. They could die here, nobody finding their bodies in the dense jungle as bugs crawled in and out of their joints. Signs would be posted everywhere searching for three lost cousins. Her face would be on the back of a carton of milk for years. And who would water her plants?

"Here it is, Wren. I got it." Daphne leaned back, handing over the damn nugget. Wren clutched it to her chest, feeling stupid for freaking out over a rock. Her best friends studied her with concerned eyes.

Her chin dropped. "Sorry," she said. Her chest ached knowing the horrible situation they could be in.

Lilah's arms reached around her, soon followed by Daphne's. They hadn't had a group hug in a while. That showed how much life had come between the girls. Nobody said anything. They didn't need to.

Wren's heart knew her two besties were dealing with life the best they could. Being single and twenty something wasn't easy. But just like in their younger years, as long as they were together, they'd make it through. Maybe not completely unscathed, but alive.

"Lilah?" she said, still in their group hug.

"Yes, Wren."

"Your shoulder is digging into my boob. It's going to pop."

"That's okay. You got another one big enough to replace the other."

For some reason that struck her as funny. Her giggle turned into a laugh, becoming a cathartic guffaw.

Lilah patted her shoulder. "Yeah, you're gonna be fine, cuz." Lilah turned and stared into the thick, lush, jungle-like terrain. "Let's see if we can figure out where we are."

Wren heard a shuffling sound off to the side. She turned to see someone, or something, scrambling through the ferns away from then. "Did you see that?" she said to both ladies.

"Yeah," Daphne said, "what was it?"

"I don't know. It wasn't very tall," Wren whispered.

"As long as it was running away from us, I don't care what it was."

"Yeah, it was probably nothing. Let's find someone with a phone."

CHAPTER TWO

Not believing what he saw, Xenos lay among the jungle foliage a short distance from the three females, watching them through dense brush, as they stumbled through the floating circle and fell to the ground. He wasn't sure what to think of them.

Portals were powerful magic only the mother goddess could create. Were these three goddesses like Mother and were they coming from the Mother's homeland? Did they have incredible magic beyond anything seen in the dimension?

Their coverings hid half their bodies, strange things protected their feet. He picked up their words here and there, but the way they bickered, then flipped and showed compassion to each other was mind boggling. He never understood females when he was younger. He was sure not much had changed on his part.

A smile came to his snout—something that had never happened. Nothing had happened worth smiling for in two hundred cold moons.

He studied the females. He'd never seen fae of such colors as the three. The one with the thin body was so pale, she looked ill. Her hair too— barely a color at all, it was so light. The bigger one had skin like the children before turning darker as adults. Then the last one, the one who had fear in her, was a rich shade of cocoa. Creamy and smooth. He wanted to rub himself all over her. She could pass as one of his people.

He shook his head. No, no, no. They weren't his people, nor had they ever been. They wouldn't claim him even if he walked into their tribe. They'd force him to leave, yell and throw rocks at him. His chest hurt. He got to his paws, shaking off the fae emotions. Animals didn't have heartaches.

He paced, still hidden by trees, vines, and ground cover. He felt. . .weird inside. Anxious suddenly, not wanting to remain still. His heart pounded harder. Something was wrong. He continued observing the females to see what they would do next.

The one who had fear radiating from her was highly interesting. Something about her drew his eyes. Her dark hair flowed like water over a fall. Her face was the most beautiful he'd seen.

Movement across the blasted ground caught his eye. The kappy. Dragon shit, it was supposed to have been his early morning meal. The little bastard scuttled away. This was the creature's lucky day. He was more interested in the trio of females.

They stood at the edge of the scraped dirt, staring into the jungle. Again, they argued, none of them able to finish a sentence before another one spoke. They almost sounded like children that needed to be spanked. An image of the fearful one, naked and under him, flashed in his mind. His cock buried inside her.

He froze. Paws locked in place. Never had a thought like that crossed his mind. Not the entire five hundred cold moons he'd been alive.

He should leave. Go away and not seek them out. Let Fate have her way with them. His eyes stared at the one with creamy skin. She was so. .

.perfect. Perhaps he'd just wait to make sure nothing happened to her. His terrain was deadly.

He wondered if they came from the Crystal Kingdom. Legends from his childhood raced through his mind. Crystal Kingdom and the beautiful forests, the castles of stone and wood the fae kings and queens lived in. They roamed wherever they wanted, whenever they wanted with magic so strong, they could stop time. And open portals to faraway dimensions.

Mother of the Land created the only portal in their dimension when she saved their world from the dark magic. These three must know the goddess. Maybe he wouldn't eat them. But he'd follow them. Try to learn why they were here. Yes, that was a good idea.

Early on, as they traveled through the jungle, he figured out they were not hunters. With as much noise as they were making with their mouths and feet, no creature would remain nearby. Unless it was hungry, looking for prey.

The females had a bad habit of reaching out to touch the flowers. Didn't they not know of the dangers lingering all around them?

He hurried forward, keeping a parallel path to theirs, but far away enough they wouldn't see him through the plants. With his black fur and yellow streaks that blended into the environment, he could walk next to them, and they wouldn't notice him.

They were coming up on the floret that spit poisonous darts. He never worried much about the flower since the stingers weren't strong enough to penetrate his thick fur. But these fae—he took a deep breath—strange smelling fae, didn't have a protective pelt.

The female lead was going to brush against the danger if she kept her current track. He scooted ahead of them, crossed their path and slapped the stem to the ground. The dart dislodged sideways, shooting straight for his nose. He dove sideways, hitting his head against a tree. Dragon shit, that hurt.

His eyes searching for further danger, he spotted a ptheragon on a thick branch high over-head. The bird's beady eyes followed the potential meal thrashing through the underbrush. Its spear-sharp beak—easily as long as his tigron body—opened slightly, preparing to pierce a fae through the belly. Its feathers ruffling as it readied to plunge.

As soon as the females passed below, the ptheragon launched from its high hiding place. Damnation. He had to time it just right, or the bird would zip by and stab the last fae. Sitting back on his haunches, his leg muscles tensed. His heart pumped so fast, he couldn't count the beats. His eyes tracked the beast.

The bird's body streamlined, wings tucked back. It whipped past branches and tall grass. Just before the beak reached the target's back, he sprang. Claws extended, mouth open, ready to chomp on a bird neck, he flew through the air. He slammed into the fluffy body, cutting off its victory cry on the first chord. They crashed to the ground and rolled into dense ferns.

He heard the females scream and run off. Mouth filled with feathers, he tried to spit them out, but many stuck to his tongue and lips. Then a sharp pain in his flank turned his head. The bastard bird had poked him in the ass with its pinpoint beak. Seeing that the bird was as big as he was, he batted its head and jumped away.

It squawked at him, no doubt angry, and flew into the branches. He continued along the path the visitors were on, needing to catch up. Before he shook off a feather stuck to his lip, a warm squishy blob splattered on his back. Then he smelled shit.

Bird shit. In the air directly above, the bastard bird squawked a laugh and flew away. Piece of kappy shit. He didn't have time to stop to get it off. No telling where those fae had gone.

He smelled his way to them. The one scent in particular enticing him forward. He didn't want to lose it. Ever. It made his insides feel light, almost like he was a cub again. Playful and mischievous at the same time. And damnation, if he wasn't smiling again. What power did this fae have over him that affected him so profoundly?

He heard heavy breathing ahead and slowed to find a place to spy from. The group had stopped.

"Anybody see what that thing behind us was?"

"It was big, whatever it was. It made enough noise to wake the dead."

His female wrapped her arms around herself, fear coming from her again. His female? That sounded right. Suddenly, he wanted to be there beside her. Be the one with his arms around her. He wanted to comfort her. But he knew this animal would only scare them more. He'd been this way for so long, he didn't recall what he looked like before the battle.

One of the girls wrinkled her nose. "You smell

that?" The others sniffed. "Smells like someone took a dump nearby."

A dump? He wondered if they were talking about him.

"I wish we had some water." Each of the girls was sweating in the heat.

"Let me wring my shirt out for you. I can't believe how humid it is. And the sun is just coming up. Grandmom is going to be so pissed."

"How long do think until we find civilization, Wren?"

"Lilah, Daphne, I hate to tell you this," the one called Wren said, "but there aren't any jungles in the United States."

The one with the bigger hips groaned. "Dammit, I knew this felt wrong. What do you think Daph?"

"I feel that way too." The one who must be Daphne whispered. "I've never seen leaves so big and so many plants in one place."

Big Hips sighed. He guessed she was Lilah. "Let's port back to Chelsea's and wait for Grandmom to get us."

He caught the scent of worry from the group. They formed a circle and stretched their arms out. Something sat in their hands, but he couldn't see what. Each female touched their fingers together and stood there. After a quiet moment, they looked around. He didn't see anything. What were they doing?

"Let's try again."

He slinked around to a different angle to get closer. Again, they put their hands out, and he noted that each held a small rock they touched together.

"It's not working! Wren, make it work."

"Me? I don't know how it works."

"You're the smart one—"

"This isn't brains. It's—"

"Calm down," Lilah said. "We just need to remember exactly what Grandmom did. Did she say any words or make any moves with her hand or head?"

Wren, his female, sighed. He almost felt her frustration. "We didn't say anything the first time. Why would we now? But I didn't see Grandmom do anything, but she could've done a spell in her head."

"Great."

"How are we supposed to know what she chanted? Whose idea was this?"

His striking fae came toward him, her eyes

watching the ground as she walked. He lowered to his belly and slinked back. She passed right in front of him. Her scent was sweet and mouth-watering.

"Hey," she said, "have you noticed the color of the trees?" She rubbed a hand along the bark. Oh, what he would do to be that piece of tree. "They're black, not brown. I wish I could've seen this before we stepped through the portal. I wouldn't have gone through."

"Wren," one of the females said, "now is not a time to be tree hugging."

He loved her name. *Wren*. Beautiful.

Wren grabbed a hold of the lower branch and pulled herself up. His jaw dropping, he couldn't take his eyes from the beauty in the tree. The way her muscles rolled and bulged, her graceful move from one limb to another.

From there, she looked around. He didn't know what she expected to see. But, hopefully, it wasn't the snake big enough to swallow his tigron farther up in the tree.

He didn't think the females would take seeing that too well. If it moved, he'd have to scare them on.

"I don't see any signs of people anywhere." She

climbed down and slipped on her shoes she'd taken off earlier. He breathed a sigh of relief. What would he have done if she injured herself? "What do we do now?"

He lay in the ferns, watching, wondering where the females intended to go. Could it be they were lost? Why did they come through the portal if they didn't know where they were? His nose picked up the scent of overwhelming fear. Wren was bent over, hands over her face. Her breathing was quick and shallow. What was wrong with her? Whatever it was, he'd fix it.

He rose to his paws to go to her, but she darted away. The other two females hollered, then chased after her. He followed, wondering what was happening. His head still ached from hitting the tree when dodging a poisonous flower stinger.

He came upon her standing in front of a white flower whose open blossom was as tall as she was. He needed to scare her away before she got too close. That flower would bring her a very painful and long death.

CHAPTER THREE

"Hey, guys," Wren hollered over her shoulder. Upon seeing the gigantic majestic flower, her panic attack vanished. She'd never seen anything so beautiful or huge. She felt like an ant standing next to it.

The stem wasn't strong enough to hold such a large blossom up, so the flower itself had tipped to the side, one of the petals resting on the ground. From top to bottom, it spanned about her height. The snow-white petals looked velvety soft.

The center of the flower had a round disc that looked shiny, almost like plastic or metal. She'd never seen anything like it.

She stepped closer, taking a deep breath, wondering if there was a scent.

"Holy shit," Daphne said, awe in her voice. "It's as big as I am. How can a flower be so large? It's beautiful."

Lilah said, "I bet that's why it's tipped over. Too heavy. I feel like the size of a bug next to that."

A play she'd seen a long time ago popped into her head—*Little Shop of Horrors*. Specifically the talking, man-eating flower character.

"Does it smell?" Lilah asked.

Wren stepped up to it and sniffed. "No—" The round stigma in the center opened, and a tongue, like that of a frog, shot out at her. Stumbling back, she screamed, throwing her hands up to block her face. The sticky tendril wrapped around her arm and yanked her forward. She continued to scream, not believing this was happening.

She looked at the middle of the flower and saw the opening had expanded enough to swallow her whole. Spikes popped up around the center, red liquid dripping from the tips.

A few feet from the mouth, her survival instincts must've kicked in, as her heels dug into the ground to stop her movement. She pulled back, the tongue stretching a bit.

Behind her, she heard her cousins scream, but they could do nothing to save her. This was happening too quickly. As she leaned back, trying to pull away, the majestic white petals snapped closed, shoving her toward the needle spikes.

All she could do was scream and close her eyes to not witness her own death. This was it for her. Her dreams of becoming a famous romance writer forever gone because a fucking flower ate her. Now, she didn't care who watered her plant. It could die as far as she was concerned.

A deep growl, like from a lion or tiger, surprised her. Had that come from the stem? Then before her eyes, the center opening with the tongue crushed as if something heavy had landed on it from the outside. The petals smashed against the ground, no longer holding her in, but the sticky thing still had her arm.

On top of the mushed flower, a dark tiger with colorful stripes ripped at the petals with massive claws and teeth.

The tiger roared, scaring Wren soundless. Nothing came from her throat, nothing went through her mind, except she was going to die as tiger lunch instead of blossom brunch. One wasn't better than the other.

The tiger's snout lunged at her face, teeth sharper than a vampire's, not that she'd seen one before. Her body cringed, and her head ducked into her chest.

This was it, a second time. She was going to die in some jungle, thousands of miles from home. She waited for the pain, the razor claws to dig in and pull out a chunk of her. Her heart pounded in her ears, and she held her breath. When she realized nothing had happened, she looked up to see the tongue flailing and flapping in the air like a ribbon tied to an oscillating fan.

The tendril around her arm was severed from the main mass. Had the tiger done that instead of attacking her? It purposefully saved her? Even now fighting the flower to get her free.

Her shirt yanked up as one of her cousins pulled on her, yelling to run. She didn't have to be told twice. Shaking the disgusting worm appendage off her arm, she sprang up and ran.

Green leaves from other giant plants slapped her face as she scurried blindly. Roots and ground vines tore at her flip-flops and wrapped her ankles. She had no plan on where she was going. *Away* was the only goal.

From somewhere in the distance, she heard her name, snapping out of the initial terrorized haze she was trapped in. When her logical side kicked in, she realized her cousins were calling.

"Marco," she said, stepping in their direction. Once used as a fun game they played in Grandmom's yard, now became a means to save her life.

"Polo" came back.

She adjusted her path. "Marco."

"Polo."

They were so close. She heard the noise their stomps created. Then Lilah's beautiful face came into sight through elephant ears leaves. Lilah grabbed Wren, then squeezed her in her arms. Never before had she been so happy to see them. Daphne joined in for another group hug. This one needed much more than the previous.

Lilah stammered through tears, "Oh my god, Wren. I thought you were dead—"

"When the petals closed. . ." Daphne said, "Oh my god, Wren."

"And the tiger," they said together.

"It came from fucking nowhere. I swear." Lilah pulled back to look into her face. "I thought it was going to attack us while some damn plant ate you." Lilah smashed her against her again.

"The tiger actually saved me." She lifted her arm to see tiny sucker indents in her flesh.

"What?" Daphne said.

"Come on," Lilah tugged on her. "We should keep going. The tiger could still be after us."

Wren looked over her shoulder, searching for a flash of color. She didn't feel the same about the animal as her cousins. There was something about it that wasn't normal.

Its eyes. . .white lines starburst from the black pupil, they looked at her as another person would —with purpose and intelligence.

"I hear water," Daphne said, and they changed direction. Wren was happy Lilah was guiding her. She was still partially in a daze from the near-death experiences.

Her world rocked again by the sudden change in environment. She went from overgrown plants, to tree trunks stretching too damn high for her to see the tops. The lowest "leaves"—fern-like fronds —were ten feet up. She could almost see a line where the trees started and the jungle ended.

"There's a creek," Daphne hollered. Lilah pulled her down a gradual slope.

"We should follow it," Wren said.

"Why?"

"Because people congregate around water for

basic survival. Somewhere we will see a town built up around it."

"That's smart. I agree," Lilah replied.

It wasn't that it was "smart." To Wren, it was common sense. All her towns and homes in her historical stories had a creek nearby. She glanced over her shoulder again, seeing jungle butt up to trees. No tiger. Disappointment touched her heart.

What the hell was wrong with her? That tiger would've eventually eaten her. It was a wild animal. When it lunged at her, it probably just missed and bit down on the tongue. A shiver raced through her, thinking of the snake-ish thing.

Daphne led them, following an existing trail. Wren couldn't help but wonder what happened to the tiger. Was it okay? She shook her head. Of course, it was okay. It was fighting a plant. A plant that ate people. And spikes with poison dripping out of them. Shit. She came to a stop, turning.

Dread filled her. Something bad was happening. Something she had to stop.

"I'm going back," she hollered on the run. Her flip flops made movement a bit difficult, but she hadn't lost one yet.

Behind her, she heard her friends yelling at her.

No, she didn't know what the hell she was doing. Following her gut was as close as she could call it.

Shortly, she saw flashes of color between bare trunks. She slowed, making sure the animal wasn't tracking them. Peeking around, she didn't see anything, so she continued. Getting closer to where they had come out of the jungle, she glimpsed the tiger lying on its side beside the creek.

It was injured. She didn't know how she knew. More gut feelings. Her feet slowly moved her closer to the tiger. She'd swear an invisible thread was pulling her directly to the beautiful creature.

Over halfway to the flowing water, she heard Lilah whisper yelling her name. She waved for them to stay back, not taking her eyes from the beast. Its chest rose and fell quickly, as if panting after a long run. If the animal had to fight that much, then she would've been toast. As she approached, its breathing hadn't slowed. Something felt wrong.

Just a few feet away, she saw the problem. One of those needle-like things was stuck in its side. A blue stream colored the pale fur from the puncture to the ground. She had no idea what the blue was, but she had no doubt the spike wasn't good.

Approaching behind the tiger's body, she couldn't see its face. And she really longed to see it. It chuffed, jerking its body. She froze.

"I won't hurt you," she stepped forward, "I promise. So please don't eat me." She wasn't sure why she whispered. It was as if she didn't want her voice to bring more pain to the creature.

"I'm right here, so don't be afraid." Was she talking to an animal or herself with that line? She crouched next to the furry back. The fur looked so thick, so soft. Temptation almost had her running her fingers through it. Instead, she carefully plucked out the long thorn then stuck it into the ground, point first.

The tiger's breathing slowed, but it didn't move or make any noise. Was it dying? A shot of fear and sadness turned her stomach. She didn't want it to die. She scooted down to the front end, leaning forward to view its muzzle. Its eyes were closed.

Her cousins went into another tizzy, this time actually yelling for her to get her ass back there right now. But not yet, she had to help.

The animal's tongue draped over the side of its mouth onto the pebbles of the creek, like when needing water. Maybe it was trying to get to the creek to drink, but didn't quite make it. She glanced up and down the stream, seeing an elephant-ear-sized leaf floating from the jungle.

She hurried a few steps, getting her shoes wet as she reached for the leaf. Again, moving slowly, she sidestepped past the back legs, no claws extended. She let out a relieved breath. Then she noticed its eyes were still closed. Was it sleeping? Should she get her ass out of there like her cousins were demanding?

One of its eyelids slid up, staring right at her, but it didn't move. Her body froze, a strange feeling shooting from her chest. She wouldn't doubt she was having a heart attack at this point.

"I'm going to get some water for you to drink. Stay calm." Yes, that last part was for herself. She squatted, cupping the leaf, filling it with liquid. One more step, and she was within eating distance, but she no longer felt any fear. Her heart was peaceful, and she felt like she knew what she was doing.

Ha, was that a joke? This was paranoia for sure.

She knelt to hold the leaf where its tongue hung. The head lifted and it lapped the water. The white starburst eyes held steady on her. They were so astounding, pulling her in. After a moment, its head rested on the ground. It chuffed again as if saying *thanks*. Or was that just her putting human traits to a nonhuman being?

She'd written a dozen stories where her tigers were half human, half animal. Shifters—that's what they were called. Maybe she was dreaming that she was the main character in one of her stories where the shifters were tigers. Sometimes she wondered if she'd lost herself too much in her fictional worlds.

The last several months, she'd been deeper than usual into her worlds. Perhaps that was why she was having more problems facing real-world problems. There were so many issues in real life, she quickly became overwhelmed and crumbled into a worthless bump on a log. It all came at her so fast, so strong, she couldn't handle it. Her own worldbuilding was the only way she could cope.

So, the human traits she thought she saw in the animal were in her own imagination.

The tiger took a deep breath and let it out, closing its eyes. She studied the injury with the blue streak. If it were red, then she would've said it was blood. After glancing at the feline face to verify it was out, she scooted closer to the wound.

Matted fur covered the area, making the puncture impossible to see. She went to the creek, refilled the leaf, then poured it over the area. After a few more washings, most of the blue was gone. She went to a knee again, leaning till her nose almost touched the strands.

This time, water was blocking her view. The fur was waterproof so the liquid clung to the animal. Dammit.

"I'm going to brush off your fur, so, again, no eating the doctor here."

When her hand touched the dark pelt, a shock stung her so hard, it knocked her back onto the pebbles.

As she sat shocked, the tiger focused on her and let out a deafening roar.

Shit. After all this she was still getting eaten. And not the good kind of way.

CHAPTER FOUR

Xenos stumbled out of the jungle into the forest. He needed water badly to flush the toxin of the flower's spikes from his system. He had only a short amount of time before his body started shutting down.

It had been years since he tangled with one of those damnation plants. After watching a ptheragon snatched from a tree by the plant's tendril and swallowed whole, he did his best to avoid them. Not that he was overly worried about being eaten, his claws would get him free. The protective skewers around the mouth with their poison were the issue.

And rightly so since one stuck out of his side,

and he was about to die. It was placed at just the right spot where he couldn't reach it to pull out with his teeth or paws. His vision became blurry, and his paw caught on a root, nearly tripping him. Dragon shit. This was bad. But he'd never regret coming to the rescue of his mate.

Yes, that was what the beautiful woman was—his mate. Took him a bit to figure it out. The sudden intense and wild fantasies playing through his head were a big clue. An animal erection was the weirdest thing he'd ever experienced. He tried to remember what it felt like in two-legged form, but the buried memories were too difficult to bring up.

He smelled the water—he couldn't see much more than smeared colors. His head was so heavy, hanging down as he panted for air. He was surprised dirt hadn't piled up on his tongue from dragging it.

His foot caught again, this time sending him face first into the small stones along the side of the creek. A grunt burped out of him when his large mass hit ground. He didn't feel water flowing around his fur. He hadn't gone far enough. Now he was going to die unless the Mother sent him a miracle.

It had been a lengthy time coming. He was ashamed he'd been allowed to live so many cold moons, while those he'd killed died so long ago. He wondered how long his solitary existence would continue. When would the Mother find forgiveness for him in her heart? The question was more *if*.

He didn't deserve it. What he'd done was beyond absolution. The blue blood on his hands would never go away.

With his head on the pebbles next to the creek, he waited to die. Slowly and painfully. Then his ear to the ground picked up an unsteady thumping, as if someone was stepping closer, but very tentatively. A voice floated through his dying haze. A beautiful sound lifting his spirits.

Wren?

Was she here? Why had she come back? His breathing was too shallow to get her smell. His survival instincts were calmly telling him that someone was coming up behind him. Normally in this situation, his body would be tensed, ready to chew off a head or arm. But his tigron knew, as he did, who this female was to him.

She came around and stared at him. He scented her fear, but stronger than that, she emanated

47

concern, care. He remained motionless, not that he had much choice in the matter. She pulled out the thorn. At least the pain between his ribs had stopped with that.

Then he watched as she snatched a leaf from the water and cup it in her hands, letting it fill with water. What was she going to do with that? If she poured it on his fur, it would just roll off. When she approached his face, shock rolled through him. Not even an insect would put itself in such a dangerous position. One swipe of his paw could break her bones.

His mate knelt before him, offering the liquid in her hand. If his maw wasn't already opened, it would've been seeing this. The bravery she showed humbled him. She was willing to risk her life to save a deadly creature.

Well, he'd put a stop to that when they were mated.

Wait. That thought had really passed in his mind as if lounging in the sun. No panic or denial rose in him. Then his mind went blank when he lifted his head to drink. He swallowed as much as he could, not only to flush his system, but to keep her so close to him. He hoped she had arrived soon enough.

His doubt and feelings of worthlessness vanished. After two hundred cold moons, this was the first day he wanted to be alive. And, of course, he was going to die. The gods had to hate him for what he did. To show him the one born for him then not allow him to touch her. He let out a deep sigh.

Her words were so adorable. There was no way he was going to harm this female. Now eating, that was a different idea. Images of her cocoa skin bared to him, his hands touching every part of her. His hands. . .

They were gnoleon fae hands, not his tigron. Fear shot through him. That part of him didn't exist any longer. It died along with everyone else he killed. But his mate was in that two-legged form.

No, not even for her could he go back. It had been too long. He doubted the magic that once lived in him was there. He gave up that privilege when he abandoned that life. He wouldn't know what to do in gnoleon fae form. His tigron was his life until the goddess had mercy on him.

His vision had started to clear. At least he could see her one last time. She refilled the leaf and poured it over the wound from the spike. When she repeated the action twice, the last time with a frustrated huff, his tigron smiled. She was so delectable. He wanted to pull her to himself and never let her go.

He saw her hand touch his fur.

Fire ripped through him, burning his insides. He roared with pain, joints pulling apart and snapping back together. Flesh tearing and re-mending. His muzzle pushed into his face, whiskers sucked in. All his fur was retreating, as if trying to hide from the world. After a short time, he lay with his gnoleon head on the creek pebbles where his tigron once was.

Everything in him hurt and throbbed. What the hell happened? He looked down at his body. His brown skin once again saw the light of day. Something he vowed he would never let materialize again. So much for that. Obviously, the Mother had been merciful, forgiving him for his unpardonable act.

That, or this was her way of making him suffer more. Was his mate a hellion?

A cramp in his stomach jackknifed his body. He rolled onto his knees as liquid spewed from his mouth. Red slime, mixed with water, made a puddle before him. His body was cleansing the poison from his system.

Now he understood why he was alive. When his body changed from one form to the other, the foreign material was extracted. He'd thrown up the toxins just then. The only other question he had was why had he changed. Even with fighting it, he couldn't stop it, and it hurt like hell. He had been his tigron much too long.

He dragged himself the short distance to the creek and washed his mouth out then sipped on the refreshing water. Seeing mud on his forearm, he licked it and realized his mistake. Yes, he'd been in tigron form for so long, that he'd forgotten how to be a gnoleon fae.

He splashed water on his tongue to wipe the mud off then onto his arm to clean it. This was going to take some getting used to until he could shift back. Right now, he hurt too much and was too weak from the poison to change. Relaxing here to gain back his strength seemed like a good idea. But what about his mate?

His tigron roared for him to get his gnoleon ass up and find her. Thinking of her thrilled him, but he didn't know what to do with a mate besides the obvious. He wasn't even sure if that part of himself worked. It'd been two hundred cold moons. Fear and shame rushed through him. No, maybe he was better just waiting here.

Looking around he saw something he didn't recognize. He scooted over and grabbed it and sniffed it. This belonged to his mate. Her smell wrapped around him, reminding him how at peace he was when she was there beside him. He'd never felt that calmness in his heart. That was what his mate did for him. Gave him the courage to believe that he might be forgiven one day.

He had to get this back to her. Maybe it was important. The thin flat material was squishy and the stretchy things at one end were of strange material. He had no idea what it was for. But that didn't matter. He needed to find her and give it back.

Remembering the terror on her face when he roared from his body beginning the shift, he wasn't sure how she'd react to him. His tigron scared every creature he'd come across. Especially the damnation kappies.

On his hands and knees in the orientation his body was used too, he realized, again, he wasn't in tigron form. Gnoleon fae walked on two feet. Holding his mate's possession in one hand, he climbed to his feet. Straightening, his head began to spin, and his balance was thrown. He stumbled to the side, kicking up water as he fell into the swift current.

This wasn't going to be a good day.

CHAPTER FIVE

Wren ran for her life, seeing huge shark-like teeth in the tiger's mouth swinging toward her. Her two friends were ahead of her, starting their run from where they hid behind trees while she tried to help the tiger that saved her life.

Now that she could look back on it, she was certain that rescuing her was what the big cat was doing. The way its white starburst irises locked with hers was strange and. . .thrilling. Or that could've been because she was trying not to be eaten by a plant. But she read the expression on its face—fear, concern, intelligence of what was going to happen to her.

No, dammit. There she went again projecting

human traits onto an animal. Perhaps she spent too much time lost in her worlds.

She didn't know what happened back there. A shock, like touching an electric fence, jolted her when her hand brushed its fur. As far as she knew, only certain aquatic life had electrifying ability. She and her cousins must've portaled deep into the Amazon jungle where humans had never been.

Earth did not have flowers the size of a small car that ate people. That thought startled her, making her stumble on stones and fallen branches along the creek's banks they were following. Were they not on—

She caught herself before falling into the water, stubbing her toe on a rock and cursing. Seeing her shoeless foot, she startled. When had she lost her shoe? She was so scared shitless trying to get away before she was eaten a second time, that she didn't notice.

"Don't stop," Lilah hollered back to her. "We're not that far away yet. It might be looking for us. Thanks to you for pissing it off."

That bitch. Lilah was in rare form today. Wren hollered back, "I did not piss it off. It was hurt."

"So what do you do?" Lilah asked, rolling her eyes, stopping "You put water on it."

"So?" she shot back. She was helping the poor thing.

"Cats hate water, Wren," Daphne hollered, grabbing Lilah's arm and dragging her forward. "Keep running, you guys. Come on."

Oh, she hadn't thought of cats and their reaction to water. Breaking into a jog, she padded along, not wanting to catch up with her cousins yet, but not wanting to fall behind either. She wasn't ready to move on. Being so close to the creature her fantasy writing life revolved around was surreal. Tiger shifters were her life, more so lately as she found the real world harder and harder to face.

If she could find a man like the ones she wrote about, she'd snatch him up so fast, his head would spin. That was the problem though. They existed only in her mind and in black ink. She'd never find a man she was happy with because she set the bar so far over their heads, they could barely see it, much less reach it.

A sharp pain radiated from her bare foot up her leg. She cursed again, this time going to the ground and grabbing her foot. In the sole, a tiny piece of wood pierced the skin. Clenching her jaw, she pulled it out.

"You okay?" Lilah asked, concern in her voice. Wren sighed. That woman was a rollercoaster when it came to making her madder than a cat caught in the rain then turning around and filling her heart with love. But she wouldn't have Lilah any other way.

"Yeah, I'm fine. Just stepped on a branch or something."

"Where's your shoe?" Daphne asked.

Wren jacked her thumb over her shoulder. "Back there somewhere." She scooted closer to the creek, lifting herself onto the rocky edge and dipping her foot in and promptly yanking it out. "Shit, that's cold." It didn't feel like that when she put her hands in earlier. She leaned over and splashed water on the bottom of her foot, washing away the blood.

Something floating in the middle of the creek a few yards up caught her eye. When she looked up, her jaw dropped into her lap. A gorgeous man riding the current toward them stared directly at her. Just before reaching her, he grabbed onto a boulder sticking up, slinging himself to the edge, kneeling at her feet.

She gasped seeing his eyes close up. They had a white starburst around the pupil. Just like the tiger's. That must've been a thing here, wherever they were. Her mind didn't work at the moment, as she stared at the work of art within touching distance.

Was she fantasizing and lost in her own head? "Hey, Lil, Daph, you guys seeing this?"

"Yeah," Lilah squeaked. Her two cousins had stopped.

The man's body was perfect. A soft brown, just like hers. Black hair hanging in wet strands around his chiseled jawline. His teeth were freaking dazzling.

He glanced at her feet, one with a shoe and one without. Then he lifted his hand in which he held her other shoe. She gasped. She saw his mind put two and two together, and he gently cupped his hand around the back of her ankle and slid the shoe on, so her toes slipped under the flip-flop loops.

His hand was chilled from the water, but heat from his touch warmed her like nothing else ever had. She felt like Cinderella at the end of the story with Prince Charming putting the flip-flop on her foot while the two stepsisters gazed on in jealousy. Her heart was stolen. Yes, he was perfect for Prince Charming.

"Thank you," she managed to get out. "I didn't know where I lost it."

When he spoke, the timbre in his voice sent chills down her back. So deep and rich. Too bad she didn't have the slightest idea what he said. Her thoughts about being somewhere in the Amazon were looking more possible. His little loincloth/diaper outfit matching exactly what she'd think a native would wear.

She smiled and he stopped talking, just staring at her. "I'm sorry, but I don't understand your language. But thank you for finding my shoe." She pointed to her shoe and lifted her foot. He continued to stare, unmoving in the water.

"Um," Wren said, glancing at her girlfriends down the way, "I have to go. We're looking for help." She got her feet under her, and when she put pressure on her injured foot, pain jabbed her lower leg again, and she sucked in a sharp breath, hopping onto her other foot.

In a blink, Mr. Stunning eyes and body was out of the water and lifting her into his arms, cradling her against him. Her arm ended up around his neck, and her other hand against his chest. His flesh was hot despite the cool water he'd been in.

Her mouth opened and closed, but no words came out.

Was this for real? No, she had to be dreaming of her next book. Stunning men didn't come out of the water and scoop her up into their muscular arms. Then he pulled her closer as if to kiss her. And she was sure as shit going to let him. Just like she would write it.

Except instead of kissing, he leaned his head to her shoulder and sucked in a huge breath, filling his chest pressing against her.

Hmm. She'd never been sniffed before. She wasn't sure if it was romantic or scary. He pulled back and his eyes were hazy. He whispered beautiful garble to her. "Vi estas mia edzino kaj mi por ĉiam protektos kaj amos vin." It sounded so sexy and relaxing. She wondered what he'd said.

He carried her toward her friends. She could barely take her eyes from him to glance at them. When she did, she giggled. Both girls stood with wide eyes and open mouths, staring at her Prince Charming.

He gave them a nod and said more words. Her cousins looked at her. "Do you know what he's saying?" Daphne asked.

She scowled. "You know I don't speak anything but a few words of Spanish."

Daphne's star-struck gaze turned back to him. "Only the cuss words you picked up at school." Wren rolled her eyes. That was not true. . .completely.

Everybody stood silently staring at each other. Well, if this wasn't awkward. Just showed that no matter where she was, being around a gorgeous man dropped her IQ fifty points.

She wiggled in his arms. "You can put me down—"

"Ne," he gruffed out, tilting his head to the left. More words flowed out as his arms smashed her to him. Okay then. She'd stay right where she was. Who was she to tell the hunk to not touch her?

Lilah looked at her. "Ask him if he knows where we can find help."

Her eyes popped wide. "Me? I don't know his language any more than you do."

Daphne grinned. "Yeah, but clearly he likes you for some reason."

She wasn't sure she would call this "liking." It verged on the cusp of creepy.

"Jes," he said with a head tilt to the right.

With surprise, the girls glanced at each other. "Did he just say yes?" Lilah asked.

"He could have," Daphne said, "but yes to what? We didn't ask a question."

He scowled and mumbled with his head down. Then he leaned over, gently setting her on her feet. He put a hand to his chest. "Xenos," he said then tapped his chest again.

Wren did the same. "I am Wren."

His eyes softened toward her, and he put a hand on her cheek. "Jes," his head tilted again, "Vi estas Wren." His touch was a surprise, but it was warm and sent a wave of calmness through her. The way he looked at her, she wanted to believe he cared for her. But that was impossible.

"Hey," Lilah said, tapping her chest, "I'm Lilah."

"And I'm Daphne."

He repeated both of their names. Then his face returned to a grimace as he ran his fingers through his drying hair. Her fingers wanted to do the same thing. She clasped her hands behind her back to avoid the temptation.

He kept mumbling to himself. She was frustrated also, not being able to communicate. He stopped, put his hands on his hips, and looked at each of them, still frowning. He put a hand on his chest again. "Xenos. . ." All she understood was his name.

He scooped her again creating a squeak from her. With her in his arms, he smiled and kissed her on the forehead. She had the distinct feeling he was laughing at her. She'd see how he felt the next time a strange woman picked him up without any warning. Jealousy streaked in her heart. She didn't like the idea of any woman touching him.

Well, shit. Dammit, she always did this with her characters. Fell in love with them almost instantly. That's what she took her jealousy to mean—this person was hers, and nobody had better lay a finger on him, unless they wanted to be in her next book and die a gruesome death.

She swallowed the emotions rising in her, as he carried her past her cousins. He looked over his shoulder, spoke, then continued forward.

Wren leaned back so she could see the girls. "Come on. I think he can help us."

Lilah huffed. "Why is he carrying you? What makes you so special."

She smiled. This was an opportunity she couldn't resist. Her friend walked right into this. "Because he can't carry someone with such a big ass." To her credit, Lilah laughed along with her and Daphne.

"God, I stepped right into that, didn't I?" Her older cousin's eyes scanned the backside of the man. "You know, I think I like this view much better. Wren, you don't know what you're missing."

Wren inhaled sharply, glancing at his face which remained neutral. She couldn't believe her cousins would say that out loud—Wait. Yes, she could. Thankfully, he didn't speak English.

"Oh yeah," Daphne added, "the narrow piece of material barely covers the goods. He might as well as just take it off."

"Woo-hoo," Lilah twirled her arm in the air. "I got a five. I'll slip into his G-string if he'll come over here and shake that thing." She continued to cheer like she was at a male stripper show. "Come to mama, sweet cheeks." She reached toward his ass and squeezed her hands as if she were testing the globes' muscle tone.

Daphne replied, "I wouldn't mind licking this entire side of his body. I bet he'd taste gooood."

"Oh, nice idea, Daph," Lilah said to her. "I like the way you think. Do you think he'd go for a foursome?"

Wren couldn't hold back the laugh. Her head tilted back, then she glanced at him. His cheeks, on his face, were bright red. His eyes were as big as tennis balls.

Oh my god, she thought. No way.

"Hey, Lilah," Wren said leaning back, but keeping her eyes fixed on his face, "how about we all get naked and go swimming."

His eyes bugged out, jaw dropping, as he glanced at her. "Oh my god," Wren said louder than she wanted, "you understand every word we're saying, don't you?"

Behind her came a duet of "What!?"

CHAPTER SIX

Xenos carried his mate in his arms. Exactly where she would always be. She was perfect. Even her toes were adorable. When he told her "You are my mate and I will forever protect and love you," he meant it. Too bad she didn't know what he promised her.

He never would've guessed that flat thing was a shoe. Whatever world they came from was much different than his.

That was never more evident than with his frustration in trying to communicate with them. He didn't understand why he knew what they were saying, but they didn't comprehend what he said.

They had confirmed what he figured—they

were lost and looking for help to get back to their home dimension. He knew where the closest help was, but it was a distance, and he vowed he'd never go back there.

He had to decide if he was going to give them the assistance they needed, or just scoop up his mate and run away with her. He knew how to survive here, obviously. They didn't need a tribe for protection or community. His tigron would hunt for food.

Pterodactyl piss, he had to do the right thing. He'd picked her up again so she would be closer to him. Have her hands on his skin. Her palm was warm, heating his insides even more. His tigron wanted out to take their mate now. Brand her to them so she would never get away. But he wasn't doing that. He'd already made one decision that could've gotten the females killed.

Goddess, that frightened him almost beyond what he could take. He hadn't made a decision concerning anyone but himself since he began his life as a savage animal, stalking the forest for his next meal. Having no responsibilities that affected others' lives. And here he was doing it again.

He would take the three to the tribe where they

would be safe. Then leave before anyone there saw him. He'd be done with them then. Go back to living like the savage he was.

A flow of sadness rolled through him, and his tigron roared. They were not leaving their mate behind. He would stay with her no matter where she was. His tigron said he needed to pull his shit together and move beyond the place he was stuck in his mind.

Panic and anxiety peeked into his head. His heart began to race. His little mate was talking with her people following them. He could put her down right now and run, changing into his beast and disappearing deep into the—Wait. Was he hearing correctly?

Were the females talking about his body? Never was he going to walk around without clothing on. What was a G-string? The thought of his mate licking him all over sent all his blood rushing below his stomach—except for what remained in his heated cheeks. Goddess, what kind of females were her friends? They sounded like a bunch of men working when the females weren't around. A foursome of what?

The next question from the delightful package

in his arms then told the females that she wanted to get naked. His knees nearly gave out. He glanced down at her. Did she really want to do that? The water might be uncomfortable for her body. He didn't know much about her system, which he would remedy when they were alone.

She stared at him with big beautiful eyes, a half smile on her face. He smelled happiness, embarrassment, and caring. "Oh my god," she said in his arms, "you understand every word we're saying, don't you?" Behind him, the females squealed like a bird when its feather was plucked.

He tilted his head and said, "Yes, of course, I understand you. The problem is you don't know what I'm saying." She laid her head on his shoulder. Her face radiated heat. Was that normal for her species?

He wondered if she still wanted to get naked and go swimming.

"Are you shittin' me," Lilah, he thought that was her name, said. What a strange thing to say. How would one shit out another person?

"Okay, stop." His mate wiggled in his arms to get down. He complied with her wishes. The three gathered around him, eyes narrowed, fists on their hips. Why did he feel like this wasn't going to be an enjoyable moment?

Lilah pointed at him. "You understand us?"

He tilted his head to the right. "Yes. Sometimes I have no idea what you're talking about."

"Yeah, yeah, yeah," the female waved her hand in front of her face, "whatever. So why don't you speak English?"

"English? Is that your language where you come from?" he asked.

Daphne emphasized. "Eeengliiish."

He repeated. "Eeengliiish."

"Yes, but no," Wren said, shaking her head. What did she mean by that? How could it be both? His frustration pounded him.

Wren threw her arms up. "Everybody just be quiet. I need to think." He watched as the area between her eyes crinkled and brows pulled down. She was so cute. Of course, she could be completely under a cover and still be desirable.

She turned to him. "Where are we?"

"You're in the Banleth Forest," he replied.

Daphne leaned toward his mate. "I didn't hear a name in all that. Did you?"

"Okay, Xenos. Just say the one of where we are," she clarified.

"Banleth." He let out a sigh. This would take damnation near forever.

"Banleth?" Lilah said, wrinkling her nose. "Where's that?"

Wren turned to him. "What country are we in?"

"Country?" He didn't know what that was. "Gecire," he said, opening his arms wide.

The females gathered among themselves. Lilah whispered. "Is Geeshire a country or a hobbit home?"

"He's too big to be a hobbit," Daphne said. "Plus, hobbits didn't look that good." She eyed him. His face heated.

His mate hit the female's shoulder. "He can hear you. Pay attention."

Daphne frowned and rubbed her arm. "I am."

Wren huffed. "Doesn't matter where we are. Someone with a phone has to be relatively close."

Lilah bit on her bottom lip. "Think loincloth hottie knows what a phone is? I bet we're in Africa, deep in Brazil."

"Brazil is in South America," Daphne told Lilah.

"Whatever. I didn't take geography in school."

He picked up on the increase of Wren's heart rate. He smelled fear from her. He laid a hand on her back. "Wren?"

"Shit," Daphne said, "she's going into another panic attack."

He stared at his mate, watching her deteriorate. He wrapped his arms around her and lifted her as he stood straight. In a soft whisper, he told her, "I've got you, my love. I will protect you from whatever frightens you." Her body shook.

He remembered a song his birth mother sang to him when he was young and frightened when a bad storm would blow through the forest. The words were long gone, but the melody remained in his heart. He hummed as he drifted side to side.

Memories from his childhood rushed forward. Good memories, times before he became a killer. He swallowed those thoughts. Now his mate needed him. He glanced at his mate's friend. Both of their mouths hung open, their eyes bouncing between him and his mate against his chest.

"Damn," Lilah mumbled, "seems Wren got herself a hot buns Tarzan."

Her words made no sense to him.

His mate let out a calm breath. "Lilah," she said with slight irritation. She patted his chest, and he let her down. She stepped up to her friend where their noses almost touched. He didn't smell fear any longer, but happiness. He was completely confused with her actions.

Her face broke into a smile, stepped back and shook her hips, singing, "Me, me, me. He likes me. I got me a hot buns." She turned is a circle with arms raised over her head. "All mine. I'm gonna keep him. Woo woo."

She looked mighty tasty shaking her ass and he noticed something about her he hadn't until now. Her breasts were beyond full. They would fill his hand. In her baggy shirt, they bounced. She was a goddess. He'd never seen anything so amazing.

He didn't deserve her, but damnation, he wasn't giving her up. He turned away from the females, trying to keep his erection out of their view. He didn't know what their views on intimate relationships were, but he was raised with the concept such things were meant to be between the couple and nobody else.

All the females wore so much clothing over their bodies that he doubted they were exhibitionist. But he had to admit that his mate would draw stares and attention by all in the tribe. Only those with wealth would be able to afford her. Unfortunately, he didn't know who those members were.

His tigron clawed at him. It would not put up

with leaving their mate with someone else. It wouldn't allow it.

Daphne and his mate raised their arms over their heads and slapped hands, all the while laughing.

Daphne glanced at him and a brow lifted. "Oh, back in school," she told him, "we had this thing where Wren was too shy to get a boyfriend, and Lilah had a new guy every weekend."

"Hey," Lilah whined, "I did not. Not *every* weekend."

His mate and Daphne rolled their eyes at the same time. He stifled a smile. She was happy with these other two. They scented very much the same —fae and elf blood, plus something else he'd never scented before. He didn't think they were immediate family, but perhaps close ties.

"So," Daphne continued, "this one time we were hanging out at a hamburger joint, and Lilah had her eye on the next weekend's guy—" Lilah huffed, "—and it turned out the guy was more interested in Wren instead of Lilah."

Lilah slapped her hands on her hip and cocked it to the side. "I wasn't *that* interested in him. And that was ten years ago."

Wren laughed. "That was the first and last time

that would ever happen. Until now." She continued to dance around, her and Daphne bumping hips. She was too delicious looking. He couldn't wait until they were alone tonight.

CHAPTER SEVEN

Wren bumped hips with Daph and laughed. The look on Lilah's face made her laugh harder. Poor Lilah, she got teased more than anyone.

She hugged her oldest cousin. "You know we're just playing around for a minute. Something to get my mind off the fact we may never get home." Her pulsed increased, her mind slipping into infinite questions that made her freak out.

A warm hand settled on her back again, calming her, bringing her back before getting to the edge. She'd hated that she came across as weak. Over this past year, she'd been getting worse. Every time too many things piled up—bills, errands, tasks—or when something happened that she had no control over. If she couldn't control her environment like she could in her books, then she started to lose it.

She was afraid to say anything to the girls because they might think she was just being over-dramatic for drama's sake and brush it off. She *was* a fiction writer by night.

"Relax, Wren," Lilah said. "When we get home, we're having a long conversation."

She scowled right back. "Yes, we are." She wanted to know what was bothering her cousin so much.

"How's your mom's OCD-ness doing?" Lilah asked. "Is she taking her meds?"

Wren turned away, shame rolling through her. "She doesn't take prescriptions, Lilah. She doesn't need them."

"That's not what my mom said last time I visited." God, Lilah sounded like an eight-year-old.

Daphne's stomach growled. They hadn't eaten since much before leaving the Crystal Kingdom. Lilah picked red berries from a bush a couple feet from the path. "You guys want to try these?" She tossed it into the air like a piece of popcorn, her wide mouth waiting for its treat.

Xenos reached over and snatched the berry in the air. She'd never seen anybody move so quickly.

"Hey," Lilah complained, "get your own."

Xenos tilted his head to the left. "Ne." He dropped the red food. He leaned forward, opened his mouth wide and made a retching sound.

"Oh, I know," Daphne said. "You can't eat the berries because they will choke you."

His head tilted. "Ne." He motioned with his hand as if pulling something out of his mouth.

"Puke," Wren jumped, "the berries will make you throw-up."

"Jes," he said, smiling at her. The girls moved away from the bush. He pointed to the ground. They looked at the spot.

"Am I missing something here?" Daphne asked. He pointed at Daphne then leaned down to put his palm on the dirt.

"One word or two?" Lilah asked. He held up one finger. "How many letters?" He looked at her with a quizzical expression. Then he held up four fingers.

"Oh," Wren said, "I was about to say you want Daphne to sit on the ground."

His excited eyes whipped to her. "Jes, jes."

Lilah frowned. "'Sit' doesn't have four letters."

Wren rolled her eyes. "Maybe in his language it does."

"But he's thinking in our language so it should be three letters."

That jolted her into a stop. Was that what was happening? He was hearing English and translating into his native tongue then answering in his language? How could he understand English but not speak it? Something was wrong here.

"Just her or all of us?" He pointed at Lilah then the ground. Obviously, he wanted them all to sit for a bit. She wasn't sure she wanted to wait much longer to get going. She only wanted to stop for a moment to give the girls a break. She stepped forward to join her cousins, but Xenos grabbed her hand, tilting his head to the left.

"Ne." He pointed at her then at himself then started into the forest. He wanted her to be with him. The girls started catcalling as her face got hot.

She pulled back, a bit worried about being alone with him. What if he was an ax murderer, even though he didn't have an ax handy? "Where are we going?"

He opened his mouth, pointed at his tongue then rubbed his stomach.

"Getting food," Lilah and Daph said together.

Oh, well she supposed that would be okay. She let him tug her forward into the forest.

"Have fun with hot buns," Lilah called out. "We'll be here when you get back."

Wren put a hand over her face, too embarrassed to look at the man dragging her with him. What the hell? It wasn't like they were going to have sex. Good God. They'd only known him for an hour. Though his hints that he liked her were rather obvious. She sucked at charades, but even she could see his attraction.

Before getting out of hearing range of the ladies, Daphne said, "Good thing the berries only made you throw up. Can you imagine how he would show the squirts?"

"Oh God," Wren mumbled. Hopefully he didn't know what diarrhea meant.

His hand was warm in hers and engulfed it. His palm and fingers were soft and smooth. He looked down at her with a smile. Her legs turned to jelly. Damn, he was so freaking gorgeous. She wondered why someone like him would like someone like her. If she were pretty like Lilah, then boys would've noticed her in school. But she wasn't. She was just plain.

He pulled her closer and kissed the back of her

hand. She gasped as his lips touched her skin. She licked her own lips, wanting another kiss but not on her hand. She smiled and shook her head. They couldn't do that yet. Hell, they shouldn't even be holding hands. But she wasn't going to take her hand back. Nope. The air was getting heavy around them. Shit.

"So, Xenos," she blurted, "the forest is pretty. So was the jungle, but I don't care to ever go back there. I can't believe no one has said much about the man-eating flower. I need to google that when we get home."

"Google?" he said.

"Yeah, that's a search engine online. . ." She stopped when she realized he didn't understand anything she was saying. "I guess you don't have a laptop setup in your tepee, huh?"

He moved his head to the side and said, "Ne."

She studied him for a second as they walked. She thought back to their charade conversations. With the words *ne* and *jes*, he tilted his head to the side. "Wait," she said, yanking him to a stop. "Your *ne* means no, and *jes* is yes."

His head tilted to the right. "Jes."

"Am I too short for you?"

He brows drew down, anger entering his eyes.

He stepped closer, his head tipped to the left. "Ne. . ." he said more, but she'd seen what she needed.

"When we say *yes*, we nod," she tilted her head up and down. "*No* is shaking the head." She turned her head side to side.

"Interesaj," he said, doing both motions.

She was so excited. She'd figured out some of his language. Granted, it was the two most basic words in the dictionary, but it was a start. She felt a connection starting. First one in the real world for a long time.

He pointed up at a tree. Leaping ten feet to the lowest branch, he grabbed a hold. Damn, that was impressive. He barely put any effort in it. She used to love to climb and sit with the wind in her hair, sun on her face. Back when she had no worries, as long as she was home for dinner.

"Kapti," he said, drawing her attention to him. He held out a ball and dropped it. Oh shit. She stepped back so it wouldn't hit her in the face if she missed. She wasn't the best player in softball. She studied the item. It looked like a yellow apple. Didn't smell like anything. He called her again and let loose of three more, one at a time.

He jumped down, landing right in front of her, startling her. Standing right there, he looked down on her. If he wanted to kiss her, this was the perfect opening. And he took that opportunity, leaning down, brushing his lips over hers. Just the lightest of touches.

Her heart flipped. So soft, so yummy. No other kiss in her life compared to the short peck she received from this man. She wanted so much more. To feel his body against hers, his hands roaming all over, touching every part of her.

She heard her voice say, "That was the most amazing taste I've ever had. Better than chocolate pudding." Her eyes snapped open, and she stared at him to see if he'd heard her. How embarrassing. He just smiled and took two apples from her hand then engulfed her free hand with his.

The sound of the birds and the breeze filled her with the happiness of being alive. The company wasn't too bad, either. He was the strong, silent type. She laughed at herself. She wasn't writing, but she felt like she was in a story, nonetheless.

"There are so many questions I want to ask, but charades aren't my idea of communicating."

"Ne." He tilted his head down then up.

"No," she shook her head, "side to side for no." He looked over each shoulder. "That's it. Maybe not so much turning."

"Will it take a while to get us to civilization, to get home?" she asked. She was already worried about what Grandmom would think. She'd never let them have the portal stones again.

He dipped his chin to his chest. "Jes."

"Really?" She didn't expect to be that far into the jungle. Maybe they *were* in Brazil. Some of his words did remind her of Spanish. She could try talking Spanish to him, but she'd probably be cussing at him and not know it.

"Will we get there today." He shook his head. "Tomorrow?" she squeaked. He smiled down at her with a chuckle and a nod. Shit. Grandmom would be furious with them.

His nose went up and he sniffed. He tugged them a quarter turn and continued. "Do you know where you're going? You can get us back, right?"

He tapped his nose and grinned. Did he mean he could smell their way back? Damn, that was like the shifters in her stories, but they were on Earth and in the real world where shifting humans didn't exist. Too bad. She let out a sigh.

He stopped at a wild bush with blackberries. He picked one and popped it into his mouth. He picked another and held it in front of her mouth.

When she opened, he stuffed it in, the back end of the bite going to her throat.

Her body jerked, bending over, as she beat on her chest. The food easily moved into her mouth where she could chew it. She laughed between coughs, totally embarrassed. Her face was so hot, she waved her hand in front of her nose, hoping the ground would open and swallow her.

Flavors exploded in her mouth, sweet and tangy. She couldn't help the moan that came out. She glanced at him, and his brows were up, staring at her mouth. Her tongue slipped out along her lips. That she didn't mean to do. Just a habit.

His eyes were wide, still focused on her mouth. God, she was really teasing him. She'd never done that with a guy before. Not sexually. After a moment of him not moving, she cleared her throat, snapping him out of his funk.

"Do you have a bag we can. . ." *put the berries in*, she thought as she stared down his muscular body with dips and hard planes, to the little bitty scrap of material that was currently pushed out, away from his thighs. She snapped her eyes up to the sky, face heating. "Nope, no bags on your body. Nothing baggy at all," she mumbled to herself.

How were they going to carry all this back? She

pulled up the front of her T-shirt, making a pouch. She'd done this all the time in her childhood, when she carried rocks home from the creek to paint. "Here, put everything in my shirt."

He looked back at her and froze, eyes seeing the exposed skin just above her waist. That hadn't been her intention, but she wouldn't change it. She liked those looks he gave her. Slowly, they were changing from fun and lighthearted to hunger and want.

Oh yes, she could completely see herself rolling around with him, coming to a stop with him on top. His hard body pressed against her, his rock-hard cock nestled perfectly where she wanted it to go. Then he'd kiss her, long and deep, tongue taking control. Slowly, he'd lift her arms over her head, holding them secured, as he took what he desired, and she wanted to give.

CHAPTER EIGHT

Xenos had finally gotten his mate away from the other two. He'd been by himself for a couple hundred cold moons, with the birds and breeze as the only sounds. Recently, the volcanic mountain range on the far side of the forests had been shaking the ground, creating a bit of chaos, but that was it. So having a group of very talkative females would take some getting used to. But for his mate, he'd listen to them all day.

Holding her hand as they walked through the trees, he'd not felt this content in a long time. His soul no longer ached with memories and guilt. For the moment, he was relieved of the weight. Just looking at her filled him with positive energy and, dare he say, hope?

But she didn't belong on his planet. She lived in some other universe. They couldn't even talk to each other. He wanted to ask her why she suddenly became afraid. Her heart would beat wildly, her body shook, the sour smell of fear rolled off her. What scared her so?

When he went to her, she calmed. Her friend noticed the change in his mate and helped her. He wondered if this was a normal thing in her life. It couldn't have been good. Was there something he could help her with? Not that he could ask her.

It took damnation near forever just to get them to sit.

But now was his chance to prove to his mate that he could take care of her, that he could at least feed her. There were many good things the Mother had gifted the land with for them to eat.

The poison berry, the female with the bigger hips almost ate, was not one of them. He'd told them it would make them sick to their stomachs, but a few berries would make them ill out the other end of the body. He did not want to try to explain *that* with actions.

Now, alone with her, walking through the

woods, all the bad things in the world were gone. She did that for him. She was so beautiful, her hair and eyes so dark. So mysterious. He wanted to take her into his arms and kiss her till she couldn't kiss any longer. Her hand in his, he kissed the back. Tasting her.

Her little gasp sent a shock through him. Had no male ever kissed her before. The thought of other males around her bothered him, but here, he would protect her from others who would do her harm.

Her voice was so soothing. She talked away, asking him questions he could answer with yes and no. Some of her words he didn't understand, but that was to be expected when two different species came together. There was a lot he didn't know about her, but that was part of the fun of getting to know a mate.

He was so wrapped up in her, that he almost missed the tree with the best fruit. After making sure she was secure, he leapt onto a branch and dropped a piece for each of them to her. She was skittish at first, but by the time he released the last fruit, she caught it with one hand.

As he pushed off the stem, his foot dragged against the trunk, throwing his balance off. He corrected himself while in the air, but he landed much closer to her than he intended. She startled but didn't step back. She stood up to him, and damnation, if that wasn't the sexiest thing about his woman.

She looked up at him with those big eyes of hers melting him on the spot. The color was a shade that didn't exist on his planet. It was so unique, just like her. And her smell was light and fresh like the air during a cold moon night.

His tigron growled for him to take their mate and make her theirs right then. No one was around to create danger, and it didn't want to wait.

No, he wouldn't do that until he knew she cared for him. Xenos refused to be that type of male with his mate, and his tigron backed off. The courting ritual was to be followed and he would comply. Starting now.

With his mate standing before him, hands holding the fruit, he dipped his head to gently brush his lips over hers. The simple kiss rocked him to his core. His heart wanted to jump from his chest, his legs would've dropped his ass to the ground if he hadn't been standing over her. His tigron kept him up. He stood straight, gauging her reaction.

She didn't move with her head tilted back, eyes closed. She licked her lips and mumbled he was the best thing she'd ever tasted. He smiled. Then her head snapped down and her eyes flew open. She stared at him as if she expected him to say something.

"I didn't say that out loud did I?"

He continued to smile and took two fruits from her hand so he could be connected to her. He felt more than a physical link starting. The mating mystery was weaving its magic around them. He wasn't going to screw this up. He'd follow the exact rules to courting so she'd never leave him.

As his mate's sweet voice floated on the air, he answered the questions he could until she asked something he wasn't prepared to hear.

"Will it take a while to get us to civilization, to get home?"

Go home? This was their home. No, his tigron whispered in his mind. She'd stepped through a magical portal from another place. Of course, she'd want to go back. But where did that leave him? He couldn't go on without her now that he'd met her. He wouldn't be able to let her go. Fear stole his thoughts, though he somehow continued to nod or shake to her questions.

How was he getting her to stay? Could he make her stay? His tigron repeated they had to claim her to keep her with them. He took a deep breath and calmed himself. They would work it out. But in the meantime, he'd show her how much she affected him.

He'd smelled berries in his last deep breath and headed that direction. The girls would enjoy the sweet bits. As they walked, he sensed the concern in her voice. She was worried about getting home. She asked if he could get them back to her friends. Didn't she know how animal's noses worked? His tigron could smell a grouse at a great distance.

He thought back to when they met. He was near death lying beside the creek. The moment he changed into his two-legged version, she and her friends had run. He didn't see her again until he pulled himself from the water and returned her shoe.

She didn't know he had two beings in one body. Another bout of anxiety erupted in his chest. Did she know about creatures like him? Would she accept someone like him to be with her? What if his tigron scared her? She'd run, and he'd never see her again. He could never tell her about his animal, who didn't like that idea.

But what else could he do? His other half said that perhaps she knew others of dual form. He wasn't sure there were others like him. Only the alphas had the magic to change. No one else in the tribe could. No, he couldn't take that chance. Perhaps they'd talk about it one day if he convinced her to stay with him.

Arriving at the berry bush, he put all that from his mind to focus on his mate. He tasted one of the berries to make sure they were ripe before he gave her one. Oh yes, almost as sweet as her kiss.

He picked another berry, and instead of handing it to her, he got close to her to feed her himself. He remembered many couples doing this when he still lived with the tribe. Being so near her was starting to test his patience. He felt his hand shake, holding the berry. When she opened her mouth, his arm jerked, shoving the bite into her mouth.

She leaned forward, tapping her chest. Oh goddess, he'd pushed it into her throat so she couldn't breathe. As she coughed, he didn't know what to do.

"I'm sorry, so sorry," he said, placing his hand on her arm as she straightened. "I didn't mean to do that."

She waved away his worry. "Sorry," she said, "I wasn't expecting the berry to be as big as it was. Next time, I'll pay attention to what you give me to put into my mouth."

Her face flushed a beautiful pink, and her arousal slammed into him. He'd never smelled anything like her. It woke something in him that had lain dormant for centuries. He needed more, so he quickly picked another berry and put it to her lips, this time making sure he didn't choke her.

When she smiled, he saw a twinkle in her eyes. She leaned forward and took the berry into her mouth, along with his fingers. She sucked on them, her tongue circling, then she leaned back, releasing his hand. Oh goddess. His patience was gone. His body was on fire for her. He could hardly breathe.

Then to make the situation harder, an incredible moan vibrated in her throat that finished him off. His world narrowed down to this luscious female before him. He wanted her like he'd never wanted anything.

Her smell, her arousal, her groan, swallowed him. He couldn't tell if his heart was still beating or not. He was upright, so that was a good sign. A deep ache rolled through his balls, his entire crotch felt ready to set fire to his clothing. A feeling like hunger tightened in his stomach, but he was hungry for only one thing.

His mate's curves were what he wanted to nibble on, to suck like she had his fingers. He wanted to slide into her hot core and bury himself until she cried out his name. A sensation—it was hard to put into words—slinked up inside his chest. Like an itch, but he had no means to scratch it. Goddess, he felt like he could die from sensory overload.

She made a noise and he snapped out of his hazy, euphoric stupor. But she wasn't done trying to kill him. She said something about a sack, then her eyes traveled down his body, taking in every muscle. He stood a little straighter and tightened his stomach. His alpha pride was sneaking up on him. He pushed that away. He couldn't let those powers reemerge.

When her eyes shot to the sky, and her face turned even pinker, he chuckled. She was affected as much as he was. Damnation, he needed to shake off the yearning eating him inside. He wasn't sure how much longer he could hold on. The woman had to stop being so sexy. The only way to do that would be to hide her under a mound of dirt, but then he'd think that was the sexiest dirt pile he'd ever seen.

He picked handfuls of berries and wondered how they were going to get these back without having to hold them. He glanced at his mate, thinking about how he could ask her, but his mind was blasted.

The woman had lifted her shirt just high enough to show a swath of her skin. Just the curves he wanted to run his tongue down on his way to more desirable areas. His hands started to fist until he felt liquid running down his wrist.

Oh, right. He was holding juicy berries.

Her arousal floated on the air. He breathed deeply. She was killing him. Yet she seemed so calm and innocent, keeping her smile in place.

Well, maybe he'd help her along in the area of expressing herself.

CHAPTER NINE

She saw Xenos breathe deeply, and his eyes flashed white as if the starburst around the pupil exploded. From where he picked berries, she saw a devious grin spread on his face. Oh shit. What had she done? She hadn't known him long enough to understand what those eyes said.

He stepped up to her, so close that his abs pressed on her hands holding her shirt, and the apples in the pouch smashed against her stomach. His scent was intoxicating. She could feel his body heat from where she stood.

He stared into her eyes, his filled with desire. She swallowed hard. He lifted his hands. He was going to grab her face and kiss her the way he wanted.

Her heart raced. She wanted this too. His hands came up to hers holding her shirt, then he opened his hands, dumping the berries in and stepped back and around the bush.

In her dazed mind, she couldn't figure out why his lips weren't on hers. His dazzling smile snapped her back. She sucked in a deep breath, eyes super wide. "You were teasing me. On purpose even."

His head tossed back, and he let out a hearty laugh. She could only grin at the goofball. He winked after his laughing fit was over and went back to picking berries. He mumbled in his language, which sounded sexy and deep. She could listen to it all day.

He dropped in another handful of edibles then held his hand out to her. She fixed her shirt in one hand then touched her palm to his. A thrill shot through her. This was turning out to be a good day. She took a deep breath in through her nose. She scented perfumes that were so much better than anything you could buy. She pulled Xenos toward a tree and sniffed the bark.

It smelled so good. Sort of like the trees at

home, but nuttier. Her hand rubbed down the bark. It was smooth, not bumpy like she was used to. Xenos called out, and she turned back to see why. She giggled at the sight.

Acorns poured from the branches, bouncing off his head. The limbs shook as if a big machine had grabbed it to shake. She held her hand out as more and more fell. "Thank you," she hollered into the air, laughing with delight. How cool was this? Higher in the air, wind must've gusted for a moment, gifting them with the tree's output.

Xenos wore a big smile on his face. He spoke and looked at her. She had a feeling of what he said —well, she knew what she would be saying at this point.

"I didn't do anything. Just being my normal tree hugger."

He gave her a quirky expression. "Arbohakisto?"

Her ears picked up "arbo" which happened to be very close to "arbor" which meant tree. Not only did she love losing herself in her stories, she loved using words. Big words, tiny words, strange words. Here was a whole new language for her.

Xenos scooped up a handful of acorns and pushed them through the small hole in her makeshift pouch that existed with all the material wrapped in one hand. She noted they weren't exactly acorn-looking, but close enough.

He held two nuts in his hand then made a fist. She heard the shells cracking. Damn, that was impressive too. His fist opened, and he picked out the good pieces, laying them on his fingers. She took a few and put them on her tongue. They tasted like pecans. Those were Daphne's favorite food. She'd be thrilled to have these.

Her shirt stretched low with an abundance of food. There seemed to be enough to feed an army, but all the bites were little.

Xenos snapped his head around, gazing into the forest. She didn't hear or see anything out of the normal. His lips spread into a smile. He glanced at her, opening his mouth to say something, but not a word came out. Not that she'd understand anything anyway.

Then he reached up and pinched her lips together. A laugh busted them apart, and he tipped his head to the left. "You want me to be quiet?" she asked.

He nodded and took her hand again. They scurried farther into the woods, coming to a mound covered with leaves and groundcover. He pulled her down and helped her peek over the top. With a belly full of berries and nuts, she had a problem staying low. He frowned seeing her struggle.

When she saw what they were there to see, she forgot about her load. Two fur babies were playing while their mother lay in the late morning sun. They roughhoused and tumbled, looking barely old enough to walk. They were so cute, her heart hurt because she couldn't hug them against her.

The creatures looked like a mix of the big cats —lioness, tiger, jaguar. They didn't have stripes like a tiger, but spottier like a jag. But the mama's fur was a smooth tan with small splotches of dark and light color. The perfect camouflage for the environment.

Then the fur balls turned their attention to their mother. They batted at her tail that smacked them around, knocking them over when they tried to grab it, bit at her ears, and climbed onto her to jump off her back.

Wren, with one of her hands holding her T-shirt's cargo, knelt against the grassy mound's incline, balancing on one arm. When she wobbled, Xenos reached out to steady her, and his hand slid over her exposed lower back.

A stream of shivers coursed up and down her, making her body tremble and breath hitch. She glanced at him to see the touch had affected him just as much. His eyes were molten gold with desire. His hand stayed on her flesh, heat radiating from that spot to her legs and up her torso.

He was so close, nearer than she thought. It wouldn't take much for her to lean forward and press her lips to his. But he had other ideas.

His palm slid across her back to cup around her other side. He pulled her down onto her side to where her body lined with his. She still held her shirt up with the food. Seemed he had the advantage with her hands unable to fight him off, if such a silly idea ever crossed her mind.

His fingers slid under her shirt and splayed over her stomach, pressing her against his hard body and cock. Fuck, his dick felt so good rubbing between her ass cheeks.

He mumbled as he placed a kiss on the side of her neck. Her body shivered in response, a zap of wanton desire streaking down past his hand, into her core. She felt her undies dampen. He gave another kiss under her earlobe at the sensitive spot. Her heart pumped wildly.

His hand on her stomach inched lower until his

pinky grazed just under the waistband of her shorts. Talk about teasing. She sucked her belly in allowing him to go lower. His hot fingertips glided along the top of her undies.

Spooned against her back, his nose pushed her chin up, and his lips sucked the length of her collarbone to her throat, where his tongue traced the skin to her mouth. He rolled her onto her back and a few of the acorns fell out. She didn't care, but his nimble fingers left her waistband and plucked the dual offenders off the ground and back into her pouch. How he accidentally grazed her breasts in the process, she had no idea.

She raised her chest, dropping her shoulders, hoping he would find something else to put in her carry-all. He didn't find anything to add, but he did find his way under the damn shirt that she wanted out of his way.

His hand rubbed over her skin until his hot digits pressed against the underside of her breast, his thumb sliding up between her mounds. Hell, yes. Chills ran down her side and one leg. She needed him to cup her and tweak her hardened nipples to relieve some of the fire burning in her channel for him. But the bastard kept his palm flat over her ribs and slid around the perimeter.

She was ready to growl at him for the long, intense tease, but his tongue was in her mouth. And, dammit, her hands had to hold her shirt or everything would fall out, which was sounding more appealing by the second.

Damn, she was going to ignite if he didn't do something. She'd never been this needy with any other male. And never had a male moved so slowly at this point of making out. Usually she was the one applying the brakes, pulling his hands out of her pants and off her boobs. Now, she could barely get him to touch her. Why was he holding back? His stone hard dick said he wanted it.

On the other side of the mound, where the fur babies and mama played, a squeal to rival any emergency vehicle echoed, startling her and Xenos apart. A low, deep growl just on the other side of the mound scared the shit out of her. The tiger/jaguar mother had snuck up on them and was about to attack her and Xenos.

Instead of eating lunch, they were about to become it.

CHAPTER TEN

Xenos popped up to see what was happening on the other side of the berm they lay on. The mama had her cubs tucked away, while she had slinked closer to the mound he and his mate watched from. Not directly at him, but to the side where a kappy was running from them.

Was the kappy spying on him and his mate? Why hadn't he smelled the creature? He was deep into his mate's arousal and hunger, but he should've been protecting her still. He had to be more careful from here on. His stupidity couldn't be the reason she died.

He reached his hand down to help his mate up, while he watched the kappy and beast to make sure they didn't get too close to his mate. When she didn't take his hand, he glimpsed down at her. What a sight!

She was stunning with the flush to her cheeks and her hair messed around her face. Her chest rose and fell quickly, jiggling her incredible breasts. He'd never seen anything so alluring. He wanted to bury his cock and face between them, lick the moisture created by their lovemaking. He would be the luckiest male in the jungles.

He scooped her up instead. When she was in her arms, she saw the mama chasing the short two-legged creature. The little thing made the huge shrieking noise.

"What's that?" she asked.

"Kappy."

"Never heard of one of those before. Must be another thing like the man-eating flower that the world doesn't know about."

He carried her off the mound, as she situated the load in her arms. What was she talking about? The kappies had been on the planet since the beginning. His ancestors had many stories about them being jokesters and thieves who would take things and hide them from the owners. They were too small to do big magic, but big enough to irritate the dragon shit out of his people.

Something strange was going on with them lately. Seldom had they traveled from their caves in the mountains. The creatures were not the kind to go out exploring, yet the kappy he chased in his tigron form this morning seemed to be doing just that. And this was quite a distance for the creature to be. What were the little dragon shits up to?

LUZZEH PACED INSIDE the cavern that he'd taken over the day the fairy queen banished him from his throne in the Crystal Kingdom. That bitch would die for taking his magic and control over the trolls. But first he had to get back into the kingdom to do that.

During his time on this goddess forsaken planet, he'd heard the legends and mythos of several peoples. Their stupid goddess happened to be the fucking fairy bitch herself. How ironic was that?

He'd found the location of a portal out of this place on an island on the other side of the planet the natives called the Standing Stones. That place was his ticket out of this dimension—all he needed was one of the queen's stones used to open portals.

He spun around to face the kappy bowing to him. "You say there were three females?" he asked the scout.

"Yes, Your Highness. I heard a loud sound like trees being snapped and went to investigate. When I reached a spot in the jungle where the land had been cleared of all trees and vines, I saw a thing floating in the air and on the other side was a beautiful land bathed in sun with fields and trees."

"And the females?" Luzzeh asked.

"Yes, Your Highness. They were arguing and holding something in their stretched-out hands that they all touched. The first two stepped through, then they got all screaming, and then the third popped out, and they all fell to the ground. The floating world disappeared."

The story was much too similar to the three females brought to the Crystal Kingdom. It had to be the trio of queens. Two were promised to him, and he received none of them. Well, one he caught trying to rescue the king's little sister from the troll dungeon. But the bitch queen got in the way of him claiming the female for himself because the damn fae king wanted her.

He wouldn't make that mistake again. Next time, he'd just kill the woman and be done with her.

"What was in their hands exactly?" he asked the kappy.

"It was dark and hard to see, but when the women fell, one of them lost what she held. I saw a small stone bounce under a leaf."

The troll king whipped around. "Did they leave it behind? Can you find it?"

"King, sire, they looked for it and found it."

Luzzeh stomped his foot, shaking the cave floor. "I must get one of the stones. None of you have found anything powerful enough for me to use. This will be my only chance to get out of this piece of dragon shit dimension. Where did they go?" he asked.

"The killing tigron was nearby. I-I think it ate them."

The king flew down the few steps to the kappy and kicked him in the side, sending him crashing into the rock wall. "You idiot. The tigron is not a normal animal. It has intelligence which I can't say your species has."

He climbed the steps thinking where the females would be. There was a good chance they were wandering the jungle and had been swallowed by a giant snake or poisoned by a flower dart. They could be anywhere. But if the tigron came upon them. . .what would it have done? It could've eaten one or two of the females. But he didn't think so.

His one run-in with the creature was enough for him. The behemoth feline had fangs that extended past its lower jaw. And those white eyes were like nothing he'd ever seen. Plus, they held worldly knowledge even though the animal was a complete savage.

"Guards!" he yelled and two kappies, with handmade helmets hanging halfway off their heads, tripped their way through the cave opening, dragging spears twice their height. When they knelt and bowed, the pounded metal hats clanked to the floor. Their spears fell as they scrambled to recapture their headgear.

Of all the creatures on this planet, how sad was it that he was stuck with morons who had no sense of battle, who had no killer instinct. This dimension was a creation of dark magic and would've been perfect for his conquests if the fairy queen hadn't stuck her buzzing ass where it didn't belong.

The two guards settled on their knees finally. "Send Ditid to me at once."

"Yes, sire."

He turned his back to them so he wouldn't have to watch them bumble their way out. Maybe the metal armor wouldn't work, after all. Their short legs were just too scrawny. He swirled his robe around and sat on his rock throne.

"May I be excused, Your Highness?"

Luzzeh glanced at the scout on the floor where he'd kick the dumbfuck. "Yes, please get out of my sight. If anyone else comes across the females, have them report to me."

"Yes, Your Highness." The king watched with a smile on his face, as the kappy limped out of the cavern. The pissant was lucky he was still alive.

CHAPTER ELEVEN

Xenos had never been so happy as at that moment. His mate was in his arms, no one was depending on him, no one asking him to make decisions. As he carried her back to her friends, she fed him from the food held in her shirt.

Wren picked out a big juicy berry and held it up for him to take into his mouth. Instead of putting it on his tongue, she rubbed the berry over his lips, a pink flash between her lips drew his attention to her.

Those lips tasted so good. Having her body against his was amazing. Her skin was so soft, so smooth. He couldn't feel enough of her. Now he understood the draw of a mate and how powerful it was. He almost threw out the courting ritual, he wanted her so badly. Fortunately or not, the fruits and nuts they had gathered kept him from losing control. The haul held against her midsection was a good reminder of what they should be doing and what they shouldn't.

He heard her friends as they got closer. Their time alone was almost over. He had a decision to make. His insides clenched.

"What's wrong?" she asked. She would be tuned into him enough already to detect changes in him. How could he tell her he didn't want her to go? That he wanted to be with her for every breath left in him. How would he survive when she went away?

His cat hissed at him. She was theirs. She was born for them. Why would he let her go? Why would their mate leave?

He reminded his cat that he was the scariest creature in the jungle and forest and for a reason. She would run the first chance she got when seeing it. Did his animal want to be locked inside forever, never getting to roam again?

His tigron backed down and retreated deep inside. What was he supposed to do? What was the correct decision? His stomach started to churn. He didn't want to make the choice.

He stopped and let her feet down. The frown on her face made his heart hurt. He'd put it there and wanted it gone to see her smile, only happiness on her face.

To make things worse, he couldn't tell her a single thing. How perfect she was for him, how smart and funny she was, how much he wanted to hold her to ease his two centuries of self-confinement. He wanted to live for the first time in a long time—had a reason.

His little mate looked up at him, concern in her eyes. She was so beautiful. He laid his palm against her cheek, and she leaned into it, a little mewl sounding in her throat. His heart hitched.

He kissed her, hard and wild like the savage he was. He still had time before he had to let her go. Time before he reached village lands. He would make the most of it. It would be the end for him.

He pulled back and rested his forehead on hers and said her name. Let the sound roll in his ears, memorizing it, absorbing it. He breathed deeply to take in all he could of her.

"I sense a change in you, Zee. What are you thinking?"

He smiled big. They had a connection. He knew it. She could read him like the rings of a tree. But like how he'd bitten and severed the flower's tendril dragging her in, he'd have to cut what had just begun. But like he thought, he had time.

He straightened and nodded. "No," was all she'd understand even though it didn't really answer her question.

She giggled at him and he quickly changed his head's movement to side to side. Dragon shit, he'd never remember which was which. He laid his hand in the small of her back and guided her toward the creek. When the two females came in sight, Wren called out to them.

"It's about damn time," Lilah said, "Y'all could've done it twice by now."

"Lilah," Wren snapped, "don't be a biddy. We brought food so that should make you happy."

The female's brows raised. "Depends. Do you have Ding Dongs and Oreos? Double stuff?" Both women's eyes studied his mate carefully as he and she approached. He sensed tension between them —the two girls, and both of them against his mate. His body tensed, ready to snatch his mate and run if danger presented itself.

When he and Wren reached where the women were sitting, Daphne smiled and smacked the bigger girl's arm. "You owe me ten bucks. I told you."

Lilah sighed. "Fine. I'll give it to you when we get home."

Wren stopped and stared at them, anger and humor scenting from her. "What were you betting on this time, losers."

Daphne pointed at Lilah. "She didn't think you two would hook up, even partially."

Wren huffed. "We didn't hook up. Give me a break. I'm not like you, Lilah."

"Hey," she griped, "I'd like you to know I haven't had sex for two weeks."

"Ooh, two whole weeks?" Wren said as she knelt and dumped the items from her shirt. "Try months. We didn't do anything." She glanced at him with an unreadable expression. He had no idea what they were talking about.

"Oh yeah," Daphne said. "Then why are your shorts cockeyed, your lips red, and leaves in your hair?"

"Shit," his mate said, running her hand over the back of her head.

"Hey," the other girl said, "couldn't y'all have

done the deed before you picked the berries. They're all smashed. Eww."

Daphne sucked in a loud breath. "Wren, look at your shirt. Those stains will never come out."

His mate held out the bottom of her shirt, and he saw how the berries had been smashed. Dragon balls. That was completely his fault. He took her hand and led her to the creek.

"What are we doing, Zee?" she asked him. He pointed to the colored splotches on her top. "Oh, it's okay. I'll just wear this around the house."

"No," he said again. That wasn't right. He'd caused the problem and now he would fix it. He stopped at the creek's edge and splashed water onto the dirt bank. His mate turned and bickered with the other two. Something about calling him a nickname.

When he'd mixed enough mud, he sank his fingers in and called forth a bit of his magic. He wanted the dirt to cleanse the material of any non-native material. Ideally, the dirt would eat anything that wasn't part of the original fibers.

Then he filled both hands with the mud and called out for his mate to turn back around. When she did, he slapped the mud onto her shirt, patting it to make it stay, while he scooped up another handful for a section he missed.

As he bent over the bank, Daphne and Lilah screamed out laughter. For a moment, he thought they were being injured, but their smell was happy. Now his mate's smell wasn't quite as fresh. She stood with her mouth open and arms in the air. Sounds came from her, but nothing else. Since she wasn't saying anything, he smeared mud on the section he missed. That should do it.

He stepped a few steps closer to the current to wash his hands. The water was warmer than it was earlier, heated by the sun. He stood and shook his hands to get water off then turned back. Before he saw where his mate had gone to, a cold, solid lump hit his arm, quickly followed by another to his chest. He glanced down to see globs of mud on him.

"There," his mate said, "how do you like that, butthead?"

His eyes met hers. There was no anger in her voice or smell even though her face was scrunched. After a moment of staring at her, she grinned, scooped up more mud and threw it at him.

He couldn't believe it. Why would she do that?

He didn't have berry juice on himself. When all three females laughed loudly, he understood his mate was playing. Tricky, she was.

Maybe keeping her was a better decision. Or maybe not.

CHAPTER TWELVE

Wren stood by the creek and spoke with her cousins, while Zee did whatever he was doing on the bankside.

"Zee? Ooh," Lilah said, "I see we're at the pet name stage already. Y'all be shucking clothes next you know."

That thought thrilled Wren, but she'd be damned if she'd let her cuz know that.

"Just because I shortened his name to something easier doesn't mean it's a pet name," she replied. "Were you ever with someone long enough to give a pet name?"

Daphne laughed, spitting out berry juice. "She got you there, Lil."

"Yes," Lilah blurted. "Remember sugar buns?"

Oh my god, did she ever. The boy was riot and a perfect fit for her cousin. To his chagrin, she called him sugar buns because he had a sweet ass on him.

Lilah scooped up a handful of berries and popped them into her mouth. "These things are good. Healthy even."

"Don't eat them all. We should save some for tonight," Wren said.

"What do you mean tonight?" Daphne squeaked. "We'll be home by then, right?"

"Zee said it would be tomorrow before we got there." She didn't know where "there" was, but she'd told him civilization, so that meant some-place with technology.

"Well, no need to hurry then," Lilah said, stretching her legs out.

"I still want to get as far as we can today," Wren replied. "Grandmom will be pissed the way it is."

The girls groaned. They knew she was right. And they'd told Grandmom that they were adults and could take care of themselves. Wrong on both those accounts.

Lilah lowered her voice, glancing at Zee. "You know you can't keep him, right?"

Anger shot through her. "Good god, Lilah. It's not like he's a stray dog." Of course, she could keep him. She wanted him. He was perfect. Then logic kicked in. He'd lived in the Brazilian jungle his whole life—all of thirty years maybe. How would he react to seeing cars or planes? Hell, people wearing clothes. He'd be in a totally different world. Would that be fair to him?

But she sensed a connection to him. Something she'd never felt with any guy. Shit. She didn't know what to do. The familiar twinge in her stomach told her she was going down the path to another attack. Dammit. She would not be overwhelmed right now. She would figure out later what to do. Thinking of his kisses moved her from panic to panting.

When Zee called her name, she turned and saw him lean toward her, slapping drippy mud all over her shirt. "What the hell, Zee?" She stood with her arms up, not believing what he'd done. She thought he was going to clean her shirt off, not burying it. Before she could move, he patted another handful on her. Was he serious?

While he washed his hands in the creek, she got her own mud and waited for him to turn around then nailed him in the arm and chest. His eyes

MILLY TAIDEN

popped wide, disbelief in his expression. She and the others laughed like they hadn't in a long time.

He was damn adorable when he was shocked. She'd have to figure out more things to accomplish that.

He stood calf deep in the creek with his hands on his hips, staring at the blob on his chest. He looked up, raising his brows and pointing to his chest, then at her. She froze. What did that mean? Was he going to put more mud on her? Her shirt was ruined. Why not?

Instead, he waved her closer. "Like I'm going to fall for that," she said, crossing her arms over her chest. He motioned for her to wash her shirt in the water. How was she going to do that?

"I'm not taking my shirt off in front of you." The size of her breasts had always made her self-conscious in public. She'd only wear swimsuits that had full coverage and didn't show much skin. Be it good or bad, she didn't like when people gawked. Just because their own chests were flat as pancakes didn't mean she had to put up with it.

Zee moved away from the creek, winked at her, and turned his back.

"I'll watch him, Wren," Lilah hollered, getting to

her feet with a huge smile. "If he turns around, I'll sock him in the balls."

Wren caught the look he gave her cousin and broke into a laugh. Lilah was better than a dad when it came to protecting her. Especially her father, who didn't care if she was alive or not.

Daphne got up. "I'll help you, Wren. Don't get mud in your hair. That will be a bitch to get out."

That they'd learned long ago being rowdy kids. Dried mud became disgustingly gross in the bathtub. With Daph's help, she got her shirt off then they stepped a few feet off the bank to scrub it in a pool of calm water. When they finished and the water wrung out, the once clear water was opaque brown. She held her top up and was amazed.

"Holy shit," Daphne said, "it looks brand new where the mud was. The rest of it almost looks dingy." She looked down. "What kind of bleaching mud is that?"

"No kidding." Wren slipped the T-shirt over her head then felt something sticky wrap around her calf. Next she knew, she was face down in the middle of the racing current.

Twisting, she was able to get her head above the water for a breath. Whatever was pulling her was going faster than the rush of water. She tried to jerk out of the hold, but that did nothing except make the creature squeeze tighter.

Her head bobbing under, she was able to get a glimpse of what had grabbed her. The first thought was a crocodile, but her leg wasn't being chewed, and crocs rolled and drowned their food. No, what wrapped around her leg was black and looked like a squid tentacle. Needing air, she fought to come up, thrashing her arms and one leg. A gulp of air and she was back under.

Remaining calm was hard, but she had to figure a way out of this. A character in one of her stories had fallen overboard on a rafting trip with her family. The girl saved herself by grabbing onto a tree stuck halfway out. Could she be so lucky? Not if her head stayed under water.

Her body thrashed, trying to twist so she faced up. Her head bobbed into the sunlight, and she sucked in another breath and fought to stay above. Water splashing in her face blurred her vision, making it impossible to see. How long had she been in the creek? It felt like hours. Was this how she was going to die? Drowned by a squid in a fucking stream in the Amazon? Hell, even she couldn't have dreamed up this kind of demise. Her stories had happy endings.

A dark blur along the bankside ahead caught her attention. Maybe it was something she could grab onto. With no time to prepare, she shoved off the creek bed with her free leg and reached her arms out. Her body scraped along sharp points—branches—until her hands tangled in a dense clump of leaves.

She clenched her hands as tightly as she could and held on. Her head rising, she saw she was snagged in a tree that had fallen. Her hands slipped as the creature pulled on her. She screamed as she tried to keep her leg from being pulled off. Something was going to give quickly.

A flash of movement along the bank upstream caught her attention. She couldn't tell what was coming, but something was moving fast her way. Her overdramatic mind said it was death, coming to snatch her soul from its earthly confines. That was from back when she wrote dark fantasy just out of college.

Blinking her eyes free of water, she was able to see partially. A four-legged animal raced down the side of the creek, the sun sucked into its dark covering. She blinked again and the animal had reached her. It leaped an incredible distance away, soaring over her head.

Was she dreaming? Dead? She swore that was the beast that had saved her this morning from the man-eating flower. But how was that possible unless it had been following them?

The tiger looking thing landed on top of something in the middle of the creek, raking its claws on something below the waterline. She heard a high-pitched screech and tried to look over her shoulder further. Water splashed along with lots of blue slime. Several black appendages whipped out of the water. Each time a tentacle wrapped around a furred leg, long white teeth severed the slimy arm.

From a distance, she heard her name. Upstream, Lilah and Daphne were running to her. The pressure on her leg released, and she pulled herself closer to shore. Hands grabbed her arms and yanked her away from the water. The girls hugged her to them as they watched the battle in the creek.

Black chunks came out of the water in the tiger's mouth, spit to the side. The piercing squelching slowly died. The tiger slumped into the water and paddled to the shore. The girls slid to the ground, panting.

Wren let her head fall onto Lilah's lap as her cousin wiped the wet hair from her face.

"Wren," Daphne whispered, "there's something you need to know." She didn't have the strength to do much more than grunt. "You know how you're always saying it would be cool if shifters really existed."

What the hell has that got to do with anything? Lilah lifted her head and turned it. The beautiful animal who'd saved her once already crawled up the bankside and collapsed, breathing heavily. Slashes leaking blue liquid. The beast looked rather rough with its fur plastered to its body, some sticking up in all directions like funny online photos of cats getting out of a bath. But she was glad it was alive.

When its eyes locked with hers, she gasped. Those starburst eyes contained pain and intelligence. A bright light flashed, but she never lost their visual connection even when the tiger became a man.

She wasn't sure she could move, wasn't sure she wasn't dreaming. All her dreams and fantasies for years had been about her shifters being real. Especially her tigers. Now she didn't know what to think. The shift was magical, not so much physical with joints popping out and skin stretching. Magic just like in the Crystal Kingdom.

"Holy fuck," Wren whispered.

"I know. Isn't it unbelievable?" Daphne said.

"No," Wren replied, "we're not on Earth."

"Oh," Lilah said. "I thought you were disappointed that he shifted with clothes on."

CHAPTER THIRTEEN

Xenos lay on the ground next to the creek, staring at his mate staring at him. Well, the decision not to tell her about his tigron was taken out of his hands. She hadn't run away yet. That was a good sign. But he could have lost her. He let her get too close to the water. But he hadn't seen a vulgaris in three hundred cold moons. How was one in this creek?

He sat up, not taking his eyes off her. He was afraid if he did, she'd be gone.

Lilah and Daphne hugged her. "You gonna be okay? You scared the living hell out of us."

His mate nodded. She whispered something to them, but he couldn't hear it. "Daphne," Lilah said unnaturally loud, "how about we go over there and see if there are any berries?"

"Yes," Daphne replied equally loudly, "let's go do that."

Wren pulled away from her friends, told them there were terrible actors, and crawled toward him. He met her halfway, enfolding her in his arms, determined to never let her go. He held her as she cried, savoring every tear that fell onto his chest.

He sprinkled kisses on her hair, forehead, and face. He breathed her in—fear, relief, and love. She leaned back and smacked his arm. "Why didn't you tell me you were a shifter?" She sniffled. "And don't use the excuse that I don't understand your language."

His brain went blank trying to figure out how to answer her. She laughed and he relaxed, knowing she was being playful though her body screamed she was in survival mode. He thought he'd been a fun person to be around. But compared to his mate, he was bump on a stump.

She cupped his face in her hands and kissed him. He let her control this. She needed to gain her confidence back. Know that she had control of something.

"Thank you for saving me again," she said. He wanted to tell her that she'd saved him too. If she hadn't removed the spike and made his form change, he would've died. If she hadn't been a reason for him to live, he might not be.

He lifted her to straddle his lap then pulled her close, rubbing her back as he rocked. Finally taking a moment to see where they had come out, he froze. Just a few strides away was the ditch his tribe had dug eons ago to transport water from the creek to the back gardens.

They were on tribal lands. A place he swore he would never return to. Too many happy and sad memories were made here. Too many friends and family lost here. Despite all that, he knew they would take care of the girls and his mate. They were good people except when it came to him. He wouldn't doubt there were standing orders to shoot him on sight.

Goddess, he hoped this was the right decision. He held his mate tighter to control the shaking in his hands. What if the alpha killed them? What if they became sick? Would his mate ever forgive him? Would he ever see her again? What if this was the wrong thing to do?

On the tribal side of the ditch, the females who

went to look for berries were out of sight. The guards and scouts didn't patrol this far from camp, so he had a bit more time with them. So he thought until the screams began.

Wren jumped to her feet and hollered out to her friends. "Zee, they're in trouble." She took off running toward the sounds, and he followed at a distance. She glanced over her shoulder. "Hurry your furry ass up." He picked up the pace while she was looking at him then slowed when she turned away.

He heard the deep-timbre shouts of a voice he hadn't thought about in years. The boy caught between being a child and a man was now grown. He wondered what his once best friend looked like. Had he shed his chubby cheeks in favor of a strong jaw? Had his hair stayed the unusual light color it had been?

Then he wondered why the guards were so far out from the village? Before, the range they secured weren't nearly this wide.

"Zee," Wren hollered. He heard the fear and anger in her one word. She was far ahead of him. She'd brought attention to herself. Tribe guards turned toward her. Xenos slid behind a tree. Wren kept yelling and had started running back to him when a guard caught her around the waist.

She gave him one hell of a time, kicking and punching. He worried her captor would become angry and hurt her. *Just let him take you, my love.* He dodged behind trees then broke into a run to get to the other side of the ditch before someone saw him. One word full of fury and heartbreak chased him from the woods. *Coward!*

CHAPTER FOURTEEN

Wren fought the tears of betrayal, but they were too strong. She sat against a tree with her two friends, while men clothed the same Zee—loin cloth and diaper combo—stood talking about them. Most of the men couldn't take their eyes off her chest. It didn't help that her shirt was soaked and stuck to her like a second skin. She was thankful it wasn't white.

With her last breath, she let Zee know how she felt about him running away. Cowards weren't allowed. If a friend was in trouble, she would be trying to help them. She didn't get it. Why would he risk his life fighting a squid thing in water but run when people arrived?

Here she was worrying about him, when she needed to be thinking how to get her friends out of this. The main thing she wished was not to die. As long as she was alive, there was hope.

The men scooted closer and closer to the tree, most staring at her chest. "Take a fucking picture," she yelled, startling her friends. The men backed away, mumbling. The two main guys who had been talking seemed to have reached a decision. Both drew their knives and headed toward the girls.

Wren stiffened. This was it. They were going to kill all three of them. They'd never see Grandmom or their families again. In her head, she screamed for someone to save them. She hoped that Zee would come, galloping in at the last second and killing all the men, saving her. That's how she would've written it, bringing in the twist at the end, when the reader didn't think the hero was still alive.

But no Zee or tiger here. Her hands dug into the ground, one squeezing on a tree root by her leg. *Please, don't let them near us. Don't let this be the end.*

A gust of wind in the branches above them whipped the leaves into a shower, blowing into the face of the two men with blades. They rubbed the debris from their eyes, not stopping. When the men were a few yards away, one of the lower limbs swung low and smacked one of the men in the arm, sending him to the ground. A second stem did the same to the other warrior, knocking him to the ground.

One of the guys on the ground yelled something, and the rest of the men standing around suddenly turned to the girls and headed toward them. Reaching the outer perimeter of the tree, limbs and branches dipped down and beat on each of the men.

Wren couldn't believe what was happening. But what was happening? How did a tree fight off a person? The men yelped and screamed as they were hit time after time. Someone had entered the area and looked around. His hands raised into the air and the men stopped all they were doing.

When he stepped under the tree, branches swung at him. Raising his knife, he cut off the limbs as they came at him. Each slice tore into her arms. He was cutting it, making it bleed if that could happen.

"Stop it," Wren hollered. More broken wood littered the ground. "I said stop it!"

The man looked at her with raised brows and the wind in the tree quieted. What was their problem? When the man started talking, all three girls groaned. Not more of this strange language crap.

"Look," she said, "we've already been through this once. We don't understand your language even though you understand us. And, no, we don't know why."

The new man closed his mouth and looked back at the others. He turned back to the girls, his eyes stopping on Wren's breasts, eyes widening a bit. She was about over this boob fascination. She swallowed her irritation, brought on by several things, and remained quiet.

The man approached them, his dagger in its sheath, and stared at Wren's dirty bare feet. He said something and she answered. "I lost my shoes while I was swimming in the creek." She jacked her thumb over her shoulder. "That's why my clothes are wet, if you're wondering." His brow raised and his head tilted.

He held his hand out to help her up. Wren glanced at the others to get their opinion of this new development.

Daphne shrugged. "I don't see why not. I don't think they're letting us go."

"And they are all as cute as Zee," Lilah added.

Wren took his hand and he pulled her up, doing the same for each girl. The warriors walked away, the girls following.

"Hey," Daph whispered, "what happened to Zee."

Ugh. Not what she wanted to talk about. "I don't know. He ran."

"That doesn't make sense," Lilah added. "I would've picked these guys over a water monster any day. And I don't even mean it that way."

She didn't know. He ran away instead of fighting. Even for her. Boy, had she misjudged what was going on between them. Tears stung her eyes. She really had hoped there was a connection.

Lilah put an arm around her shoulder. "It'll be alright, Wren." Lilah put her other arm around Daph. "It'll be us against the world, just like it used to be when we were kids."

"Dear god," Daph said, "If we survived that, I guess we can survive this."

Wren grinned. "You're still allergic to getting hurt?"

"Damn right, I am. Y'all can fall out of as many damn trees as you want. My ass is not leaving the ground," Lilah said.

"And that's a lot of ass—"

"—to keep on the ground," they finished together. They giggled, arms around one another. The guys glanced at them now and then, but Wren didn't care. Her heart would hurt for a while, but she'd move on like humans always did. One step at a time.

Ahead, she heard voices and clanging of metals. Was this the civilization the man-who-will-remain-unnamed was talking about?

Coming out of the trees into a field of sunlight, the first thing she saw was a huge-ass garden with several people working it. She had no idea who was male or female. Most wore loin cloth diapers, a few others wore skirt-like wraparounds. And no one wore a shirt. Their cocoa skin gleamed in the sunshine.

Some wore their hair braided down the back, some had it wild and free. When they walked past a female staring at them, Wren understood their fascination with boobs.

"Uh, Wren," Daph said.

"Yeah, I get it. Compared to completely flat chests, mine would seem quite strange."

"They don't even have to wear a bra," Lilah said,

jealousy in her voice. "I would do about anything for that."

Wren snorted. "You think I wouldn't?" She watched as a person on their knees dropped a seed into a hole, covered it, then placed their hands over it. After a couple seconds, the dirt moved and a green stem popped up. It kept getting bigger with several leaves blooming from the stalk. The person then scooted over and scooped out another hole and dropped a seed.

"Did you see that?" Daphne almost yelled, turning the heads of those nearby.

"Magic," Wren explained. Like she thought when Zee shifted. This place was of magic like the Crystal Kingdom.

They passed a woman and young girl walking the main path with large woven baskets balanced on their heads. Wren stared wondering how that was even possible. With each step, no matter how her body moved, the woman's head didn't bob or jerk. As Wren watched, the woman turned and looked down at the girl, tilting her head. And the basket didn't fall! What the fuck? Was it strapped on? No—duh. Magic.

Lilah bumped Wren with an elbow. "Don't go

all panic attack right now, but didn't you say at one time that we weren't on Earth?"

"Yeah," she said. "Why aren't you freaking out about that and this magic shit?"

Wren shrugged her shoulder. "Guess that with Chelsea and everyone in the Crystal Kingdom, being on another planet and magic doesn't seem that strange anymore."

The only thing about being on a different planet that bothered her was the fact they weren't supposed to be there and didn't have a way to get back.

Off to the side, three people seemed to be bagging flour. One person scooped handfuls of those acorn-looking nuts onto a flat rock while another person rolled a bigger stone over them, crushing and making them into a powdery end product.

Another area, where several men gathered, had a hundred straight sticks that were perfect for roasting marshmallows. The men were whittling the ends into sharp points and attaching large pieces of leaves to the other side. Arrows? The only weapons she saw on the guys were long knives. Which was where the clanging echoing through the village came from.

The typical smithing tools and hot fires were set on wide swaths of dirt. There seemed to be a lot less metal than wood here. Which made sense, being in a forest.

The men had them stop, and most dispersed to individual, tall mounds of ground. These places were like tepees, but instead of tall sticks with draping animal hides, the ground was pushed up into a dome with the entrance covered with dense vines hanging down. She wondered what the inside looked like. Was this where the people lived?

Ahead of them, the rest of the village lay. The mound homes created a protected barrier area where a ton of activity was going on. Kids sat in groups learning various things. One was basket weaving with as many boys as girls joining in.

Another group appeared to be cleaning and preparing veggies, or what she thought were vegetables. It could've been battery parts for all she knew.

So many more things were happening in the center area. She felt the life in this community. Even though they worked with their hands, with not a single computer in sight, this was a civilization. But one cell phone would've been nice.

The man who had helped them to their feet

earlier returned with a female who wore thick necklaces around her neck that covered her chest. It wasn't a shirt as such, but Wren didn't feel awkward looking at her.

The woman had a beautiful smile, while she spoke gibberish. Lilah did the honors of telling her of the no incommunicado situation then laid her hand on her own chest. "Lilah," she said. Daphne and Wren introduced themselves.

The woman called herself Iridia and the gorgeous big guy was Haml.

So after everyone knew everybody's name, they just stood there looking at each other.

"May I have something to drink?" Wren asked and Haml jumped into action, probably glad to be doing something. Iridia gestured for them to follow her. As their foreign tour guide, Iridia spoke about the village, pointing out things. Some things looked interesting. She'd have to come back to find out what they were.

Their tour ended at the other side of the village where a bonfire blazed with several older folks sitting around it. Iridia introduced Wren and her friends and continued talking, as Haml handed them wooden cups filled with water. The liquid tasted just like the creek. That was probably their only source of water.

One of the older ladies got up from her seat and came up to Wren. Taking her free hand, the elder held it up and flipped it over, palm up. A gnarled finger traced the lines while she spoke. Then the woman shuffled to her cousins and did the same, except didn't say anything to them. The trio watched quietly, as the elder hobbled to a grass-covered dome.

Lilah looked at Wren. "Fortune teller?"

"Why not?" Wren replied. "They have magic. How much different is knowing the future?"

"Ask her if we'll ever get home," Daphne added. A low rumble rolled through the older group. Wren wasn't sure what to think. The ladies stood quietly sipping on their water.

Holding a small, but full, pouch in his hand, a tribesman maybe ten years older than her, with many tattoos on his torso and a fierce scowl, approached the elders. He spoke to one of the male elders. The visitor spoke first, and all the elders gasped or raised their brows—and then looked at her.

Not prepared for such attention, Wren stepped back. Lilah scooted in front of her and crossed her arms over her chest, blocking Wren's view of the newcomer. The group continued talking, the conversation becoming fervent.

Iridia grabbed the warrior by the arm and dodged the punch he threw and sent one of her own to his stomach. He grunted and stepped back, slightly bent. She grabbed a fistful of his hair and yanked his face down to hers.

Wren was scared to death for the short, but brave woman. That man could eat her for breakfast, but he didn't make another move toward her, as she chewed him another asshole. Shit, she'd do just about anything to hear what the conversation was about, besides herself. Should she be worried?

The older woman had returned, now holding a small wooden bowl with what looked like catnip in it. She stopped in front of Wren and the elder tilted her head to the side as far as it would go. Wren wasn't sure if the woman was gesturing yes or no like Zee had taught her or she just liked standing with her head sideways.

"Wren," Lilah whispered, "why is her head like that?"

"Don't know." Wren smiled and moved her head slightly in the same direction. Was this a monkey see, monkey do thing? When her head matched the angle of the elder, the woman took a pinch of catnip and shoved it in her ear. "Hey," Wren complained, returning her head to the normal position, but the woman's finger was still pressing on it.

The woman grinned. "Does that bother you?" she asked, taking her hand away.

"Well," Wren worked her jaw, trying to get the nip to settle, "it's kinda weird."

"Yes, of course," the woman said. "It will fall out in time."

Daphne poked her back, "Wren," she whisper shouted, "you're talking to her. How do you know what she said?"

Wren glanced back at Daph with a questioning expression. "She put kitty cocaine in my ear."

"Oh," Lilah added, "it does look like catnip, doesn't it? I was thinking more along the lines of crazy weed." Her cousin tipped her head to receive her *weed*. "Of all the ways to do pot in college, in my ear was never one that crossed my mind." Wren elbowed her cousin to stop talking about that stuff in front of the adults.

The lady winked. "Oh, we have much better ingredients for that than this."

Oh great. That's all they needed was Lilah and

the elders running around naked, high on pot, expressing their first amendment rights. She'd rather get back in the creek.

"How does that stuff make us understand you?" Wren asked.

"It is part of the grand magic of Gecire. Magic makes communication possible. It translates from one language to the other in your mind. When given the magic, you may speak to all."

"Well, ain't that some shit," Lilah replied. "I would've killed for this in Spanish class."

"But beware," the elder continued, "not all words are interchangeable."

"What do you mean?" Wren asked.

"If there is an item in your world that does not exist in ours, then we don't understand."

"Like if I say the word car," Lilah answered, "then you get no word for it?"

"I get the word *car* from your language even though that word doesn't exist in mine. I don't know what a *car* is. Also, if there is more than one name for something, you will hear the one you are most familiar with."

"Awesome," Wren said, "no SAT words. What good is a word if you don't know what it means. I stick to the easy to understand when writing."

As Daphne got her earful, Iridia joined them without the angry tattoo guy. "What were you discussing with him?" Wren asked.

Iridia replied, "He wanted to buy you, and I told him no."

Wren choked on the air in her throat. "Buy me? Nobody buys me. I'm not for sale."

"He thought you and your friends were captives, not guests," Iridia said.

Wren didn't know what to say. "Thank you. We would prefer to be guests. We need help."

The short woman nodded. "I thought as much. You are not from our dimension."

"What gave that away?" Lilah snorted. Wren elbowed her again. "What? I was just making a point."

Iridia gestured for them to join the elders next to the fire. Before they sat, the woman reached toward the ground with her fingers splayed, and a flat pile of dirt rose and formed into a seat. All three girls' mouths dangled open. They'd seen magic when with Chelsea and her half-sister, but still it was shocking to see.

Iridia sat on her dirt seat and smiled at them. "Welcome to Gecire," she said with a slight bow of her head. "We live in the forest of Banleth." Her arms lifted out to the side, palms up. "We are gnoleon fae. Forest ground dwellers. People of the land. Our magic speaks to the dirt and plants that we use to survive."

"Ah, got it," Lilah said. "That's how you were able to do the dirt pile thing we're sitting on."

Iridia tilted her head to the right. "Yes. I am Iridia, alpha and leader of the fae tribe. You are welcome among us as friends."

"Thank you so much," Wren replied. "We have so many questions and need help getting back home."

"Where is your home?" an elder asked.

Wren blew out a breath and looked at her companions. "I guess we should tell them our story."

CHAPTER FIFTEEN

W ren and her cousins told the elders about their epic failed adventure to get back to Grandmom's. The listeners took everything in stride, not interrupting to ask questions or giving them looks that called out bullshit. Wren left out the part about the tiger and Zee. She didn't feel he needed to be a part of it. What did he matter?

"So, here we are," Wren wrapped up, "needing to find a way to make the stones work to open a portal or some other means to get back to Earth or the Crystal Kingdom."

The older gnoleons got up and formed a circle, whispered to each other. Haml brought them another cup of water.

He said, "The three of you are like nothing we have seen in our dimension."

"You don't get many visitors?" Wren asked with a smile.

He chuckled. "No, not from off our planet."

"What's your position in the hierarchy?" Lilah asked him, batting her lashes.

Wren rolled her eyes and cupped a hand over her mouth. Leaning toward her cousin, she whispered behind her palm, "Stop hitting on him already."

Her cousin frowned. "I'm not—"

Daphne leaned closer to their eternal flirt. "You are to. You just don't know it."

"Fine," Lilah grumped. "I won't say anything until we're home."

Wren and Daph shared a look. They knew that wasn't going to happen.

Haml smiled. Wren thought his cheeks may have been a little pink under the dark skin. "I'm the alpha's second. We work together with the elders to make decisions and run the village."

Wren glanced at Iridia listening to the group of elders. "I'm surprised that your alpha is a woman. Not that I'm complaining. But in most shifter books on Earth, a male is always the alpha with another male beta."

A shadow crossed Haml's face. Wren remained quiet to see if he would explain. Instead, he glanced out to the village. "Being male or female matters little to us except for reproduction and work requiring physical strength that magic cannot do."

"That's awesome," Wren said. "I doubt humans will ever get there unless there are changes that aren't possible in society right now."

The elders adjourned their impromptu meeting and walked back to their seats by the bonfire. The woman who put magic catnip in her ear stood several feet in front of the older group and lifted the gnarled staff in her hand then slammed it onto the ground.

A vibration rose from Wren's feet, up through her legs and torso. She felt an incredible urge to get as close to the woman as possible. Glancing at her friends, she knew they felt it too by their wide eyes and bodies leaning forward as if to jump up and run the few yards to the woman.

A low roar behind her turned her around on her seat. It seemed all the children and several adults were stampeding toward them. As she watched, children of all ages crammed in around Wren and her cousins, forming a ring around the elder with the staff.

Wren felt her shirt move and looked back to see a little girl was feeling the material.

Her big eyes were adorable as she asked, "Why do you wear this?"

Wren opened her mouth to answer then closed it. Studying the crowd, no such garment was in sight for anyone else. It amazed her how different two cultures could be, yet be so similar.

"I don't want to get cold," she said, having no better reason.

The girl giggled. "The sun is always hot here. Only during the cold moons do you need to protect your skin."

Cold moons? "What are the cold moons?"

The girl looked at Wren like she couldn't believe a grownup would ask such a question. "They are the days and nights when the air turns cold even when the sun is out. They don't last very long. I am six cold moons old."

"Ah," Wren replied. A cold moon was probably what humans called a year.

The small one put a hand on Wren's arm. "No one has ever had breasts as big as yours."

Yeah, Wren could understand what the child was saying. But she wasn't prepared for the next question.

The child raised her hand. "May we touch them?"

Wren twisted so quickly to avoid the small hand, that she fell off her pile of dirt. Those around laughed and giggled. "Uh, not right now, okay?"

"Okay," the girl said, turning her attention to the boy beside her. "She said no. Only the alpha is allowed to touch her. When I grow up, I'm going to have breasts like that." The boy's eyes widened, and his jaw dropped. Yup, Wren thought, very different cultures.

The elder female in the middle of the circle tapped her staff on the ground twice. "Good afternoon, young ones." In a united voice, the kids greeted her in kind.

"Today, we have guests from far away. Their way of living is quite different from ours, so don't worry if they do something they shouldn't." The elder winked at her. "In their honor, I will recall the creation of our world. I think our story will answer many questions they have."

MANY COLD MOONS AGO, too many to count, only dust existed in the darkness. When the gods and goddesses decided to create a perfect, beautiful planet the Crystal Kingdom came into existences.

The dark magic was unhappy because the balance of power went to the good magic. So it decided to make a place where it could rule. While the gods' attention was on their creation, the dark magic spun itself a planet.

It was almost finished when one of the goddesses discovered the new location. She came to this world and let loose as much of her good magic as possible. She scolded the black magic for being jealous. If it had been more patient, it would've been included in their original creation.

But now this planet existed, and the darkness was tasked to take care of it as it would be its home forever.

Now, the parts of this world that hadn't been yet made, the good magic brought to life. The gnoleon were the first and best creation. Next came the forests of Banleth giving a home to all the good creatures while the evil beasts remained elsewhere in their misery.

Afraid that the dark magic would abandon its child, Mother of the Land sealed the heavens above so the magic wouldn't be able to port away. But she still needed to cross back into her time. The problem was how to lock the portal from the dark magic.

She created the Island of the Standing Stones. There, she set up a place where she could come to check the planet and leave without worry of being followed by those who were meant to remain in the dimension.

In the middle of the standing stones, Mother of the Land placed a magical gemstone on a flat rock and an opening into her world appeared. When she stepped through, she took the stone with her, effectively closing off the exodus point.

To this day, the Standing Stones remain exactly how she left it on the island. Those of the dark magic had tried to destroy the stones just because it was created by goodness. They were destroyed.

Since then, no one has dared to cross the water to reach the island.

The gnoleon have lived in peace with others of

the Mother's creations. We share her memory with each generation, so her goodness is worshipped and remembered. Upon her return, we will praise her and thank her for her light.

CHAPTER SIXTEEN

Wren had been captivated by the storyteller, so engrossed in the history, that she'd not noticed how far the sun had traveled. The woman was right when she said many of their questions would be answered. Unfortunately, so many more had popped up.

The young crowd sitting around them had disappeared and joined into what looked to be preparations to eat. Recalling the story, Wren remained in her spot by the fire, while Lilah and Daph were helping the children with their tasks.

Haml raised a dirt seat and sat next to her. "What questions do you have that I can answer for you?"

She smiled at him. "In our world, had you told a story like that, no one would believe it. They would call it fantasy. But here, I'm assuming it's what really happened."

His head tipped to the right. "Yes. Our creation has been passed down from elders to children since the beginning of our time."

"It was that way for a time on Earth too. When we invented the written word, stories were recorded for others to read whenever they wanted."

"The people on the other side of our planet have words on leaves. They use it mostly for tracking money when trading goods."

"There are more people here than you guys?"

"Yes. There are many species. The citogan fae live in the volcanoes in the direction of the setting sun. Dreoxbat fae stay in the swamplands closer to those who bargain and trade. There are probably others, but gnoleons have not been the traveling type since defeating the Qhasant."

"Who are they?" she asked.

Haml sighed. "Those were beings of the dark magic in the dimension's past. They existed just to bring suffering and pestilence to the inhabitants.

At that time, our village was twice as big as it is now.

"Being a peaceful race, we didn't hunt the qhasant to kill, until villagers began disappearing. I won't go into what happened to them. Just know that death would have been better than what they experienced."

Sorrow and anger flowed from Wren's heart. She wanted the qhasants to come back so she could beat the shit out of them some more. "How did you get rid of them?"

"That is a story unto itself. It is known as the battle for the life of the planet. The other fae nations joined us to wipe out the evil. Fighting was fierce. We lost many good people including our alpha leaders—Iridia's parents—and my best friend."

The shadow over Haml's face she'd seen earlier returned. "Were you alive then?" The way he talked, the fight was long ago, but his deep emotions said he had lost those he loved.

"I was barely past boyhood, not yet a man. That was two hundred cold moons ago, give or take."

Wren choked on the air in her throat again. "Seriously? How old are you?"

"Around five hundred cold moons, but some-times I feel like a thousand." He chuckled. She was having trouble wrapping her mind around it.

Haml stood and offered a hand the same as he had in the forest when he helped her up. "The meal is ready. May I escort you to your seat?"

Wren turned to see scores of tables with mounds of dirt for eaters to sit. How had that been setup so quickly? She thought back to Elgon, the new village created in the Crystal Kingdom with her other cousin Chelsea.

"Why don't you use tree roots to make chairs? You control the trees, right?"

He tilted his head to the left. "No. Only the ground and plants in it. The trees are their own entities. Too powerful for us to control. Only a true female alpha can talk with the trees. Perhaps you can show us some of your magic."

Wren laughed. "I don't have any magic to speak of. My grandmother was a queen in the Crystal Kingdom, but I'm not the one who inherited her powers."

"What do you mean?" Haml asked. "You can do what gnoleon fae cannot."

The little girl who sat next to Wren during story time ran up to her and grabbed her hand.

"Please sit with me. You're so nice," the little one asked as she pulled on her arm, dragging Wren from Haml.

What had he meant? What could she do? She'd have to get her answer later.

CHAPTER SEVENTEEN

Xenos watched the village gather for the evening meal from his position in the forest canopy. His cat would lay long days in the cool breeze and patchy sun. This high up, he was safe from most creatures. Besides normal birds, only the big snakes came and that was only for a meal worth going up for. He wasn't worth the puncture marks he'd leave behind.

He listened to the elder as she retold the story of their world's beginning. After knowing Wren's story, he saw the similarities and understood something was changing on the planet, bringing the dark magic to the surface again. That would explain the kappies roaming where they normally wouldn't and the reemergence of the water creature that took Wren.

Then he saw Wren sitting by herself, while the other two girls participated in meal preparation. She thought too much. Maybe that was the reason she had moments of extreme fear where her breathing became labored.

His eyes narrowed seeing a male walking directly toward his mate. As the man neared, Xenos recognized the pointed nose, the lighter complexion and hair. His body was strong and as big as any alpha. He wore confidence and casualness well. Something Xenos did not.

He listened to their conversation the best he could, but this height only sent him her laugh. And he didn't even deserve that for leaving his mate. He just couldn't take the chance of having the girls hurt if they were found with him. He was sure his tribe would kill him on sight.

No matter how hard he tried to keep running the other way, his body and mind pulled him to get his ass back to his mate. He'd snuck around the guards watching the outer perimeter of the village. He wanted so badly to be with her. His heart longed to be happy near her, but not even for her could he come home.

The group gave thanks to Mother for blessing the land with food and all their needs. The normal meal cleanup came next. Discarding the trash and leaving honors of sacrifice to the Mother.

Wren seemed to always be looking for someone. He didn't know who, but jealousy hit hard when he thought about Haml sitting with her, touching her hand. Would he try to claim her? His tigron clawed at him. It would kill Haml, best friend or not.

The gathering of the elders was a new change from when his parents ruled. Iridia spoke with them a few times. Other than that, they remained in their places

Xenos's sister showed the ladies a berm for them to stay the night. The mound was bigger than most, but there were three adults together. When the rest of the village had disappeared into their own homes, Xanos came down the tree and snuck to the back of Wren and her cousins' pile of dirt. Using his magic, he made a quick entrance at the back side and entered, sealing the opening behind him.

The girls first screamed when he came in, but they calmed as he went to the front and closed that entrance, pushing the small torch more toward the center. When he turned, Wren was there, throwing her arms around his neck. He melted under her touch. Just the short time away had been too much. He squeezed her to him, breathing her in. Then he took her lips with a passion that couldn't be denied.

He peppered kisses along her forehead and down her neck. He'd forgotten how good she tasted, how good she felt against him. Then she leaned back and punched him in the shoulder with the heel of her hand.

"What the hell were you thinking abandoning us with these people?" Wren said, crossing her arms in front of her chest, drawing his eyes to her breasts. His look made her hotter than she should've been.

"I didn't abandon you—"

"Okay, you ran away," Wren clarified. "Better?" He cringed at the anger in her voice. He deserved that.

"Wren, these are the people I was taking you to."

"Then why did they have to *capture* us? Why couldn't you have introduced us or at least let them know we were with you?"

"No," Xenos said, grabbing her upper arms.

"You can't tell them you know about me. Have you said anything?"

Her eyes were filled with confusion. "No. I was too mad to think about you much less talk about you."

Xenos let out a soft breath. "Good. Keep it that way. It's safer for you."

"Why is it safer?" Lilah asked. "Are we in danger right now?" She pulled her sleeves up as if ready to fight anyone who would challenge them.

"Not from anyone in the village. Only outside with the wild creatures."

"Then why are you so concerned about us?" Wren asked.

"I'm not," he blurted, frustration riding him hard. "Wren, I'm here to talk to you. I must tell you things, so you understand why I ran. Why I will continue to run. Please, love, hear me out."

Wren sucked her lip in and turned toward her friends. The question went unspoken—did she give him a chance to explain? The other two agreed, to his relief. She turned back to him.

"I want the truth and all of it, or I'm calling it right here, right now."

He sat on the ground, making it softer than normal.

"I was born around five hundred cold moons ago." He paused as the girls reacted to that. He wondered how old they were compared to him. They looked a bit younger than him but knew that didn't mean much when it came to time. After Wren closed her open mouth, Lilah returned to a sitting position from falling back, and Daphne took another breath, he continued.

"My parents were the alpha—leading—couple of the village. Back then, the village was much larger than it is now."

Wren said, "Haml had mentioned that." Jealousy ripped through him thinking about the male being so close to Wren. He tried not to show it,, but his animal made that hard. "What happened?" she asked.

"The dark magic of the world was strong then. Very different from now." Though with the few changes he'd seen lately, the balance could've been changing. "We fought an evil species who lived to hurt others. The battle was intense. The fae were losing. So many died." His heart squeezed at the memory. He didn't want to recall what he'd spent hundreds of years suppressing.

But for his mate, he'd do almost anything. He hit his chest with the heel of his hand and cleared his throat. "Somehow, a group of fae, including my parents, were cut off from the rest of us. They were surrounded and taken down." He hadn't seen their deaths. Didn't need to, to know they were gone. During the battle, an anguish took him to his knees tore through him. Then he knew.

"It became my decision how to proceed. I'd been three hundred cold moons, barely an adult, when the conflict began. Too naïve to the way of things and consequences. In my anger and grief, I made the rash decision to continue the fight. I wanted revenge."

The image in his head of the aftermath of his choice stole his breath. So much blood, so much death. Brown, red, and blue mixed into one burial ground. Wren scooted behind him and wrapped her arms around him, laying her head on his back. He leaned into her, needing to feel as much of her as he could.

"So many died. All generations lost loved ones. Our village dwindled to so few. All because I made the decision to go on."

Wren lifted her head, leaving a cold spot on his back from the absence of her warmth. "But you won, Zee," she said.

"Did I? Did we?" No, he couldn't categorize so many deaths as a win.

"Is that why you were in the jungle?" Daphne asked.

He nodded. "I was too ashamed, too devastated, at what I'd done. I didn't deserve to be the next leader of the gnoleon. I wasn't worthy, so I ran. I shifted into my tigron and vowed to never return to my fae form or the village. That was my punishment for my failure as a leader."

"But, Zee," Wren said, stronger, "*you won*. What would your world be like if you stopped fighting, and saved those lives, and they were enslaved or tortured? Would that have been preferable?"

"Of course not," he replied. But still. . .

Lilah cocked her head. "What has all that to do with why it's dangerous for us to know you?"

Was she serious? Did she not understand? "Because everyone in the village wants to see me dead."

"Why?" Lilah continued.

He glanced at his mate, hoping she'd explain what he was missing in her friend's logic. "Because I made the decision that killed hundreds of lives."

Lilah snorted. "I think you underestimate your people, buddy. Maybe you *weren't* meant to lead."

Beside him, Wren stiffened. Her face held a frown toward her friend, who was correct in her final conclusion. His mate looked around. "Is there a way we can have a moment alone? Go outside."

"No. We're not going outside. I will raise a divider between us."

"What?" Daphne sputtered. "You're going to separate us?"

Wren sighed. "Just for a little bit, Daph. Unless you want to hear all the mushy stuff."

Lilah and Daph glanced at each other. "We do," they said together.

Wren huffed as he laughed and raised a wall of dirt between him and his mate and the two girls. Next, he brought up the light algae in the ground that cast a faint glow in the smaller space. For a moment, neither of them spoke. He didn't know what to say to excuse his actions. There was no excuse.

Wren doodled with her finger in the dirt, eyes down. "I thought we had something going. I guess I was wrong."

He grabbed her, setting her on his lap to straddle his legs. "I feel it too. I didn't want to leave you when my tribe came, but I knew they wouldn't accept you as friendly with me."

"How do you know that?" she asked.

He sighed. "I just do. How would you feel if someone was the cause of your family being killed?" He stared at her lips, which he wanted a taste of. "I never let you leave my sight but for a moment at the beginning."

"What do you mean?"

"I followed from a distance to make sure you weren't harmed. When you reached the village, I climbed the trees to watch over you. If anyone threatened you, I would've sliced their throats."

Her watery eyes met his. "Really? You never left me?"

"Never." He cupped her face with his hands and kissed her with every bit of himself. "I won't ever leave you," he managed between kisses. "You're my mate."

From her position straddling his thighs, Wren pushed on his chest, breaking his hold on her. "What?"

Oh, kappy shit. Maybe he shouldn't have told her. He should've waited to learn her culture and way of things. He wasn't following the courting ritual, skipping ahead.

An unwanted familiar smell made him cringe inside. His mate's face paled, and her pulse jumped up. She choked. He didn't know what was happening, but he wouldn't let her get worse. He needed her to know this was a good thing.

He took her shaking hands in his. "Wren, I knew the moment I smelled you, that you were the one for me. Never had I been affected by a female until you stepped through the portal." Her breathing slowed. "I will always cherish you."

Her luscious lips turned down. "Wait," she said, "you saw us come through the portal?"

"I did. And I followed you. . ." he wasn't going to admit that, at first, he thought about eating them, and that now, he only wanted to *eat* her.

Her smile grew wide. "That's how you saved me from that damn flower."

"Among a few other things, yes."

Her brows drew down. "What do you mean?"

He laughed and pulled her to him. She was back to normal. Her heartbeat was steady. "Those stories are for another time. But you are my mate, and I won't ever leave you."

"I know all about mates," Wren said, excitement and hesitation in her smell, "that is if they are the same as in human lore."

"What are your mates?"

"Mates are born to be together; meant to find

each other. The Fates separated them, so they would grow and become the mate they needed to be, before they could come together as one. Once they met, each would know. Well, the shifter knows because of a smell. The human is always dumb, because they usually refuse to acknowledge what their hearts are telling them. They are afraid of rejection."

"Yes," he confirmed. "What does your heart say?" Her eyes widened. A sour tang hit his nose. "I cannot reject you, Wren. No matter what you do or where you go, I will be with you. Whether you want me or not."

She laughed. "Yup, that's what our shifters are like too. Seems some things are universal even across dimensions."

"Mother created us. She didn't invent a totally new species. She had a good model already created."

"I think she reached the top of the line here. I don't want to be anywhere but with you."

CHAPTER EIGHTEEN

Wren bit her lip and stared into the eyes of her mate, as she straddled his lap. Damn, that's something she never expected to find when she came to visit her cousins. It was strange enough landing on a different planet, then finding out about magic, and that shifters were real! Now she had one of her very own. She couldn't make this shit up if she tried…. Well, that wasn't true, she did that in her books all the time, but still!

"Wren, are you ok? Did I say something wrong?" Zee's worried gaze trailed across her face, and she smiled at him.

"You're perfect, I was just thinking how perfect for me you are. I never thought I would find a mate, I thought they were fiction, but here we are." Wren ran her eyes over the angles of his face and made a decision. She wasn't fighting her feelings or the attraction she felt for her mate.

With her decision made, she grabbed the hem of her shirt and pulled it over her head. Zee's quick inhale caused goose bumps to trail across her skin. She was nervous now that she had made her choice, his people were flat chested. Would he think she was abnormal, or even ugly, with her larger breasts?

"Wren, my mate, what is this garment you wear around your breasts?" Zee's fingers lightly traced over the crest of her breasts, and she sucked in a breath.

"It's called a bra, the women on Earth wear them. They keep our breasts from bouncing around when we move." She could hear how raspy her voice had become from his simple touch across her breasts.

"It's interesting, but I'd much rather see you with nothing hampering the view. Take it off mate." Zee's eyes were glued to her breasts, and Wren was nervous. She took a deep breath and then started to laugh when Zee's eyes got bigger, she hadn't thought about what the action would do to her chest.

She reached behind her back and unhooked her bra, but quickly grabbed the cups and held them against her body. She was afraid to let it drop, what if he was appalled at the size of her breasts?

"My mate, please let me see you. There is nothing about you that I would ever find distasteful, I want to worship every inch of your body. Let me show you." Zee's eyes burned with a golden fire, and Wren couldn't tear her eyes away. She felt his hands on hers, gently pulling them away from the material, and she let it drop.

His eyes dropped, and he licked his lips, the sight sent lust straight to her pussy, and she wanted to clench her thighs together to ease the ache, but instead she ended up squeezing his hips.

He cupped her breasts, and Wren couldn't control her moan.

"They are heavy mate, is that why you wear that contraption, to help with the weight?" Zee's fingers rubbed across her nipples, and they puckered.

"Yes Zee." That was all she could manage, there was something about having his hands on her body that turned her mind to mush. "Zee, please."

"Anything you want is yours."

"Touch me, I need to feel your hands on my skin." Wren thought she would go out of her mind with anticipation if he didn't do something.

Wren ran her hands across Zee's shoulders, loving the feeling of his muscles and skin under her touch.

"Your breasts are so responsive to my touch mate, can I taste them?" Zee's eyes glowed, and Wren clenched her hands on his shoulder.

"Yes please."

Zee leaned forward and took her nipple into his mouth, his other hand continued to play with her other nipple. Tugging and pulling on it gently. Wren moaned and rocked her core against his cock.

With a pop Zee pulled his mouth off her nipple and turned his head to the other, when he spoke his hot breath fanned across her nipple. "Thank you goddess for giving me this bountiful feast."

Wren wrapped her fists in his hair and held his face to her breasts. Her moan filled the hut, and she was thankful for the wall he had built. "Zee."

He looked up at her but never removed his mouth from her breast. His eyes twinkled, and she knew he was enjoying her torment. She smirked and used her legs to push him back, so she was straddling his prone body. The movement released her breast from his grip, and she sat up. "Stay still mate."

She scooted down his legs until she straddled his thighs, and then she leaned down, placing a kiss on the corner of his mouth. She kissed her way across his face, to his neck and then lightly down to his chest. She licked her way down his chest to his stomach and peeked up at him. "I think this loincloth needs to go, mate."

"Anything you want. Your breasts rubbing down my body as you moved, make me want to flip you over and worship the very ground you lay on." Zee's hands were clenched at his side, and she reveled in the power she held.

She sat up, and ran her hands up her stomach to her chest. "These drive you crazy?" Wren bit her lip and watched Zee's reaction to her teasing. His eyes darkened and they were glued to her hands on her breasts.

"What about if I do this...." Wren pinched her nipples and lightly tugged on them, she let her head fall back and a moan erupted from her lips. "Do you like this Zee?"

A light growl came from him, and Wren ran

her hands over both breasts, alternating between tugging, twisting and caressing them. Zee's hands came to rest at her hips, and he clenched them on her.

"Your beautiful, large breasts are mine to play with mate." Zee quickly flipped her over, and she could feel his cock against her core. His eyes rested on her hands still cupping her breasts. "Fine you want to play with my breasts... I'm sure I can find something else to amuse myself with." Zee's eyes trailed down her stomach, and she felt the path he took burning her from the inside out. She arched her back and clenched her thighs around him.

"All in good time mate." Zee ran his finger across the waistband of her clothing and gently rubbed his finger under it. "Do you have any other surprises for me?"

Wren choked out a laugh, "Maybe, I don't know the hygiene practices of your people."

Zee cocked an eyebrow at her words, and she decided not to explain what she meant. He would see when he removed her pants and underwear. Shit, did his people even know what underwear is? That alone could be an interesting surprise.

He unhooked her pants and slid the zipper

down, she watched his face for any reaction to her clothes.

"Zee, I'm wearing what we call underwear. I guess you could say it's like your loincloth." Wren bit her lip, still clutching her breasts and waited.

"This material that is so soft, holds a treasure I can't wait to see. I'm going to take them off you now." Zee glanced up at her hands and then back down to her underwear. He grabbed the waistband and started pulling them down. Her underwear went with them, and she lifted her butt to help him.

HE WRAPPED his arms around her thighs and lowered his face to her pussy. At the first swipe of his tongue on her clit, she bucked. "Oh my God," she moaned and refused to follow her body's command to shut her eyes.

HE LICKED around her waxed lips and proceeded to fuck her

with his tongue. She panted and ground her hips down, closer to his face.

. . .

"Please…"

She whimpered when he did a slow trail around her clit with his tongue. He flicked it twice, and then she felt his fingers rub up and down her pussy, wetting them with her dripping heat. Feeling his calloused fingers over her sensitive flesh turned into a new point of pleasure. After a moment he dipped wet fingers into her. She groaned. Her hips rocked on his face involuntarily.

He sucked on her clit, while his fingers curled and thrust in and out of her. It took very little for her to go over the edge. Her heart pounded in her ears, each beat a fierce, wild gallop. Tension unraveled inside her, pushing her headfirst into an all-consuming orgasm. She screamed when a wave of pleasure rushed through her.

Panting like she couldn't get enough air in her lungs, she blinked the haze of happiness away and looked down at Zee. Her insides melted at the blazing look he gave her.

"Fuck me." That had not been what she'd planned on saying, but it worked just as well.

While she watched, he gripped his cock, rubbed the tip on her pussy lips, and coated his shaft with her moisture. He slid into her in a deliberate, drawn-out move. She groaned at the slow torture. She contracted around his thick length and every inch, as he went deeper inside her.

He was big, and he stretched her in a way that made her feel every nerve ending in her pussy sigh in bliss. Once he was fully embedded in her, he lowered, his arms bracketing each side of her and caging her in.

Without waiting for his command, she lifted her legs and wrapped them around his waist, locking them in place behind his muscular ass.

He lowered his head, and their lips meshed in a wet tangle of tongues. While he kissed her senseless, he pulled out of her and slammed back in with so much force she was glad she was holding on to his arms.

Again he withdrew and thrust into her hard. And she loved it. A fine

sheen of perspiration coated their skin, and allowed him a smooth glide over her body. In and out he went. She pulled her lips away from his and moaned. Her nails dug into his shoulders, while she hung on to him for dear life. The sound of skin slapping, grunting, and moaning filled the room with an erotic melody that increased her pleasure.

"Yes, more," she pleaded. The coiling tension inside her was near its breaking point, and she needed him to fuck her harder. He quickened his thrusts until she could no longer speak and all her focus was to topple into orgasm.

CHAPTER NINETEEN

Luzzeh sat on his throne, tapping a knobby finger against his chin. "With a gnoleon," he said. "Are you certain?"

"Yes, sire," the kappy said. "They were watching two cubs and their mother out of their den."

"Ah," Luzzeh laughed, "that explains the scratches across your arms and legs." He laughed harder. The door opened, and the kappy from earlier walked in. "You," he pointed to the first piece of dragon shit, "describe to him the female you saw." The two kappies spoke, while he beat a brown-spotted fingernail against the arm of his seat. "Well," he said after a moment. "Is it her or not?"

Both kneeled and bowed their heads. "Yes, sire,"

one of them said. "I am sure it is the same female from the portal."

He licked his lips. He could smell the fairy bitch's blood already. A surge of power flowed into him. Filling him with more magic than he had in the Crystal Kingdom. He didn't know where the darkness came from. Didn't care. As long as it made him stronger, he'd accept it unconditionally.

His chest tingled with the darkness completing the hole inside where his magic dwelled before the queen took it and banished him. Thoughts of all the ways he could kill her played through his mind, none of them painful enough.

"S-sire, may we be excused?" a kappy asked. Luzzeh extended a finger toward the two, a black streak shooting from the end. The kappies vaporized. "Dismissed," the troll king said and laughed, the sound echoing in the rock walled chamber.

"Guards," he shouted, "gather the troops. We're going for a surprise visit to the neighbors."

CHAPTER TWENTY

Xenos lay beside the female he'd spend the rest of his life with. His animal was just as thrilled as he was. They'd found their mate despite his wrongdoings. She tried to tell him his decision during the battle was justified because they won the war against evil.

He couldn't accept that, could he? If the tribe didn't, he didn't. Forgiveness had to be earned.

He wasn't sure when the sun cycle would begin, but he felt it would be soon. When his little mate moved, she looked up at him. Big brown eyes sucking him in. When her cheeks blushed, his heart swelled with love. He would never forget their first night together. He wrapped an arm around her and rolled her against him. Her chest to his. Her breasts foreign feeling and amazing. His tongue wanted to tease her nubs more, gently biting to push her into an orgasm.

But he'd settle for a kiss—a long, deep, arousing kiss. Maybe they had time for another round of lovemaking before he had to go. His cock hardened at the thought. Her smell during sex was so much better than when she was upset. He needed to know how to keep her from whatever caused the panic attacks.

He kissed her forehead and temple. "Love, tell me why you sometimes are lost in your fear? How can I cure you of this?"

She leaned her head against his chest. "I don't think panic attacks can be cured. At least, not mine."

"Why not?" he asked. "What creates them?"

"It's a long story—"

"I will listen to it all," he insisted.

She kissed his throat. "You are the best person I've ever met."

He wasn't sure he agreed with that, but he wasn't going to let her sidetrack him. "The story?"

She let out a deep breath. "My mom does everything to perfection and has her entire life mapped out. I mean, who plans meals for an entire month ahead of time and writes it on a calendar? She always used to tell me that if I didn't plan, I'd wouldn't get where I wanted to be. If I didn't make a list, I would miss something, and my life would be screwed up. And if that happened, she wouldn't be there to help me.

"She made me feel inadequate of controlling my life. I guess somewhere along the line, I started to believe that. When something out of my control happens, especially lately, all these questions cram into my brain, and I freak out because I know I'm going to fail, and then what would I do?"

He felt a wet drop land on his chest. He held her tighter, wanting her to go on. "Why especially lately?"

She snuggled into him. "I don't know. Maybe because I'm getting older, which means I'm getting closer to the failure she knows I will be. Maybe because life keeps piling one thing after another on me and I can't cope. Too much to control."

"What if you made that one pile of things into many piles of one thing?" he suggested.

"What do you mean?"

"What if, from your pile, you choose the most important thing and put that by itself." She nodded. He continued. "Then go to that new pile and deal with it by itself, shoving away the rest."

"Then what?" she asked.

"Go back to the big pile and pick out the next most important thing. Put it in its own pile, all the other stuff gone for the moment."

She was quiet. He wasn't sure if that was good or bad. He scoffed at himself. He was giving advice when he couldn't deal with his own issues. What a joke.

He said, "Ignore what I just said—"

"No," his mate said, "that makes sense to me." She pushed up onto her elbows. "If I focus on one thing and accomplish it, not worrying about the other things, then eventually, everything will get done, right?"

"You won't be overwhelmed, I don't think anyway."

A big smile spread across her face. "That might work. If I don't freak out and forget it all."

He crunched his abs and gave her a brief kiss. "Don't worry. I'll be there to remind you."

She pushed his back to the ground, pressing her chest to his and throwing her leg over his body. "Promise, mate?" she said with a grin, wiggling down his torso until his cock kissed her entrance.

"I promise, mate," he replied, once again, crunching his abs, his hips raising instead of his shoulders. "I promise," he breathed out as she engulfed him.

A short time later, he lay on his back, his mate breathing steadily on his chest. He thanked the goddess for bringing her into his life. He would treasure his mate for his entire life, but the sun was about to start its cycle.

He rolled her onto her side, waking her. "Sorry, love," he said.

"It's fine." She wiped hair from her face.

He pulled her clothes from under the dirt and shook them off.

Wren huffed. "Why are my clothes buried in the dirt? I have to wear those till I get home."

"I washed them for you." He noted her anger and didn't understand it.

"You washed them? By covering them with dirt?"

"Of course," he replied. "How else would you wash them?"

She stared at him with wide eyes. He laid her shirt out, perfectly white where it should've been and bright colors where called for. Next he unburied her shorts and mysterious things she wore under her clothes.

She snatched them up and studied them. "Is that why you put mud on my shirt with the berry stain?"

Ah, he'd forgotten about that. "Yes."

She rolled her beautiful eyes. "Why didn't you tell me you can make the dirt clean things?"

"Because you wouldn't have understood what I said," he answered.

"Oh, right." She slipped a see-through garment up her legs, that he wanted to wrap over his face so he would be surrounded by her smell everywhere. It even had holes for his eyes to see out. "Wish I had superpowers."

"Magic?" he clarified. "Of course, you have magic. You're my mate."

She froze with her hips in the air, pulling up the clothing. "I have magic?"

"How do you think all those nuts came off the tree at the same time when we gathered food? I didn't do that. And I saw the tree you sat under beat away the warriors who held you and your friends before I left."

"But I didn't do anything either time."

He kissed her forehead. She was so adorable when she had no idea what was going on. She grabbed the item that caressed her amazing breasts. What a lucky piece of material.

He climbed to his feet and headed to the front of the berm. "I'll be back tonight."

"Where are you going? You said you weren't leaving me." Confusion and anger lit her voice.

"Love," he said, creating the opening that had been there, covered with vines, "the tribe will kill me on sight. I won't endanger you with my selfishness."

Her face remained a frown, but she didn't say anything. On his way past her, he leaned down and kissed her hard. "I love you. I'll be watching you all day from a safe distance."

She nodded but didn't smile. There wasn't a frown either, which he considered a win. He took down the dirt barrier separating the others from them, the dirt dissolving into the ground. Her friends were still sleeping, as they should've been.

He made an opening at the back of the mound, stepped out, then resealed it. He took a deep breath to see if anyone was nearby. He heard no activity. The tribe hadn't awakened yet. He hurried away through the trees with thoughts of being buried in his mate's body racing through his mind.

His tigron sensed danger, but not soon enough. A body slammed into him, taking them both to the ground. They rolled, each making a powerplay to gain the advantage. Hitting a tree, they came to a stop. Xenos had a shifted paw and claws against the attacker's neck ready to rip his throat out.

The other male had his knife pressed to Xenos's vein, which, if severed, would kill him before he could change forms. The man snarled his name.

Xenos could only say one word. "Haml."

CHAPTER TWENTY-ONE

After dressing, Wren sat against the wall of their domed sleeping location thinking about yesterday. So much had happened, it felt like a week had passed.

So many thoughts, each having different emotions, bombed her. Being lost and frightened, being alive and grateful, being in "like" with Zee. Was that dumb? She didn't want to say *love*. What would the others think if she told them she was in love with a guy she'd known for twenty-four hours? They'd laugh and tell her it was just horniness—well, Lilah would say that anyway.

But her heart said it was more than just a temporary bodily desire. Hell, any physical cravings she would've had were satisfied after her multiple-orgasm night, and her heart still ached with him being gone.

This was almost identical to what happened with her cousins in the Crystal Kingdom. Chelsea went for a run and a couple days later, she was mated. When she asked her cousin if she was out of her mind for mating a guy she just met, she was told that was how things were. That's how mates worked.

Zee said she was his mate. And last night she believed it whole-heartedly. But if that was the case, how could he leave her now?

But if he showed his face here, they would kill him and possibly her and her two cousins. She couldn't be so selfish, that they all died because of her. That was just not happening. She'd live with a broken heart if it came to protecting her two besties.

She pulled her hair in frustration. Lilah and Daphne slept on the far side of the dome. She didn't want to wake them so early, so she got to her feet and peeked through the ivy covering the door. Only seeing one person down by the garden, she stepped out and smacked into a moving wall of rock.

She eeped and fell backward. Haml grabbed her arm, letting her get her balance.

"I am sorry for frightening you," he said.

She had a hand on her chest, her heart pounding. "No problem. You just scared the shit out of me." She gave a little laugh.

Haml's face scrunched, and he leaned to the side and looked at the ground behind her. "Do you need a change of clothing?"

Why would he ask that? Her clothes were "washed." She looked over her shoulder to see what he was looking at, then she realized what she had said, he took literally.

She busted out in a laugh. "It's just an earth saying. I didn't really poop in my pants."

I leaned back and smiled. "That's good. Seems the magic doesn't translate perfectly."

"I guess not," she replied, feeling kind of embarrassed in front of someone so manly. When he turned his head, she saw a line of blue on his neck. "What's on your throat?" She gestured toward with her head. He quickly reached up and wiped his fingers over his skin, smearing the color.

"It's just a little blood," he said.

His words shocked her so much that she froze,

eyes fixed on the cut where another drop of blue slowly formed.

"Wren?" Haml said with worry in his voice. "What is wrong?" He laid a hand on her shoulder, hot and heavy.

"Uh, I—umm, our blood is red," she answered not knowing what else to say. "I guess seeing yours is blue really made where we are sink in. Everything is so Earth-like here, it's easy to forget I'm not there." She shook her head, feeling genuinely dumb now. She wanted to go back into her sleeping hole and hide.

"Red?" he replied. "Really? I never would've thought about that."

She didn't know what else to say and one of those damn awkward moments, when neither the guy nor girl knew what to say on the first date, hung in the air.

"Would like to accompany me while I refill the water jugs?" he asked.

This was a surprising turn of events. "Uh, sure. Why not?" Perhaps he would answer some questions she had. She followed him toward where the tables with food were set up last night. With no one up yet, the tables were out of sight.

Haml lifted two five-foot tall wooden barrels

and set each on a piece of plywood-looking base with a long handle attached. He grabbed the handle and dragged it behind him. It was like he was pulling a sled along the dirt. She noted how the ground in front of them magically smoothed into a flat path, making their walk nice.

"So," Haml said as they walked the trail, "did you sleep well last night."

Oh god, did she ever after the third go-around. "Yes, I had no problems. I was very exhausted."

"Good," he replied, breathing deeply.

"Yesterday, you mentioned something about my magic. What did you mean by all that?"

Haml remained quiet for a moment, then asked, "Are you aware of your magic?"

"No. Why do you think I have magic?" she asked.

He gave her a half smile. "Do you think that tree attacked my men on its own?"

"What tree?"

"Think back to when we met. Where were you?"

She'd sat under a tree with Lilah and Daph beside her. The wind in the tree picked up and thrashed through the limbs, making them hit the men. She'd been praying for help, but she didn't mean tree help.

He asked, "Do you feel a draw to nature? Trees in particular."

"I do. I spent a lot of time hanging out in the woods at Grandmom's. My cousins call me a tree hugger."

Haml laughed. "Hugging trees is not part of magic, I wouldn't think."

Yeah, she didn't think so either. The sound of water rushing came ahead of them. After a moment, she saw the rocks along the bankside. Haml dragged the sled to a calm shallow pool beside a boulder in the water. He tipped the tall container onto its side so it lay on the ground. How would he ever get water to come up over the bank and go into the barrel?

As she watched, the ground under the container sank until it was low enough for water from the pool to flow in. When it was full, Haml tipped it back up and swapped it out for the other one and repeated the same process.

She was amazed seeing magic at work. Earth would've been so different if magic existed there. The possibilities were endless.

When the sled was reloaded, they headed back.

Haml took a breath as if to speak but didn't. After the third time, she asked if he wanted to ask her something. They came to a stop on the trail and he turned to her.

Behind her, she heard a familiar growl. Looking over her shoulder, Haml's eyes popped wide, and his hand snatched up the bow and an arrow from the quiver. Wren leaped forward grabbing the bow.

"No, don't shoot. Let me handle this." Just to make sure he didn't change his mind, she wrestled the bow from him then stomped toward the tiger several yards away. She was not going to put up with this kind of shit. Reaching the animal, she slapped it between the ears.

"Don't you dare growl at me when I'm with someone else. If you can't handle it, then stop being a pussy and show yourself. Otherwise, I will be with whomever I want. Man up or forget it." She spun and marched back to the trail then handed back the bow. Haml stared at her.

"What?" she asked, holding the weapon out to him.

"Where you come from, is that how you handle wild beasts who could eat you in one bite?" He took the bow, lifting it over his shoulder.

She laughed. "No, he's a special case." She stepped forward getting them back on the trail. "Can I ask you something?" After he nodded, she cleared her throat then loudly and clearly asked, "What would the tribe do to someone who, during battle, made an order to attack and many people ended up dying, but you won? Would you want to kill the person who made the order?"

He stared at her for a moment, then loudly he replied, "No! That's part of war!"

She smiled and returned to her normal voice. "Thank you." Then she said a bit louder into the trees, "I expect an apology or the right to say I told you so."

"I apologize," Haml immediately said.

She waved her hands in front of her. "No, not you. Someone else."

His eyes surveyed the land ahead of them. "But there's no one else here. Are you feeling ill? Maybe need some water?"

She laughed, then from behind a tree next to the trail, Zee stepped onto the path. Haml took in a deep breath, freezing on the spot. Her eyes ping-ponged between the men, then she shuffled to Zee and put her arms around his back.

She whispered to him, "Thank you for showing

yourself. I told you they didn't hate you."

Zee had his arms around her, but his eyes never left Haml's, even when he bent down to put a kiss on her forehead. "Yes, love. You were right." He moved slowly and cautiously, trying to push her to the side and behind him.

When she realized what he was doing, she slapped his hands. "Stop that, Zee. I'm safe. Haml won't hurt you or me, will you, Haml?" She looked at the man staring at her mate. Neither had said anything. Maybe they didn't know each other. "Haml, this is Xenos. Xenos, this is Haml. He's Iridia's right hand."

Haml threw his head back and laughed as hard as he could, though she didn't know why. With drawn brows, she looked up at Zee. He just raised a brow as if to say *don't ask me.*

Finally, Haml quieted, wiping a hand over his face. "Well, fuck me. You are alive. I knew it was you when I first smelled the girl." He shook his head, eyes searching the woods to the side. "Two hundred cold moons, and you decide to show up."

The happiness in Wren at her mate coming out evaporated with Haml's serious tone. She stepped in front of Zee. "I can explain," she said. Before she could open her mouth again, an arm came around from behind, fingers pinching her lips together just like before they went to see the mama and baby cubs in the woods. He couldn't tell her to be quiet, so he smooshed her lips together to get across what he needed to communicate.

Of course, he pressed himself against her back, giving her tingles and memories of last night.

Haml stepped toward them, Zee stiffening, his body tensing. Haml reached out a hand as if to shake. Zee slowly released her lips then grabbed Haml's arm just below the elbow. Haml's hand wrapped around Zee's arm. Haml then pulled Zee in for a man's slap on the back hug with her still between them. It was a bit weird, but not too unpleasant of an experience. She'd never played *let's make a Wren sandwich.*

Haml stepped back and smiled, still holding Zee's arm. "It's good to see you again, brother."

Her mouth dropped open. "Are you brothers?"

Haml smiled wider. "Not by mothers, but by choice. He is same mother brother to Iridia."

Mother brother? That was a strange transla-tion. "Wait," she blurted, "Iridia, the leader, is your sister?" She pointed at Zee. Shit. Last night, Zee did tell her he was the son of the alpha who died in battle. But that didn't register until just now. Holy shit. Zee was the king of the gnoleon. She wasn't sure if this was good or not.

She asked Haml, "Why did you say you knew it was him?"

He answered, "The first time I smelled you at the tree, I recognized a scent but couldn't figure out how I knew it. Then I realized last night. I waited outside your berm to see if I was correct."

"I'm glad you didn't kill me," Zee said to Haml.

Haml chuckled. "And I'm glad you didn't kill me, Alpha. Your tigron senses saved me."

"Yes," Zee said, "had it been anyone else, I would've torn their throat out."

Wren swallowed hard, putting a hand around her neck. Zee was big enough to do something like that. Though she'd never thought about him being a vicious killer. She just didn't see that in him, even as a beast.

"Come," Haml said, "there are many in the tribe who would like to see you again."

Wren squeezed her mate's hand, and he looked down on her. Damn, he really was tall. Only because she knew him so well did she notice the fear in his eyes.

She hoped this reunion that she instigated went well. If someone got hurt, it would be her fault.

CHAPTER TWENTY-TWO

Xenos held onto his mate's hand. She was his lifeline as he faced the hardest day of his life since leaving his people. Who knew something so easy could be so hard?

His best friend took the water sled to its place next to the food tables. The tribe was up and about preparing for the morning meal. That would mean everyone was there.

"Zee," Wren said, squeezing his fingers, "are you okay? We don't have to do this."

He put his arms around her waist and lifted her off the ground as he stood straight. "Have I told you today how perfect you are? How much I love you?"

A shy smile lit up her face. "Well, when I was on

top, and you had my tit in your mouth, you mumbled how perfect it was."

His heart and cock jumped. He backed her against a tree, her legs wrapped around his waist, and rubbed his stone hard dick against her mound. His mate was a force all by herself. She had incredible power over him, and she had no idea.

She tasted so good. The sweat and salt on her skin from their lovemaking remained. She was all the sustenance he needed. All he ever wanted.

And to be accepted by his people—if he once again became a part of the tribe, to be with those he loved and grew up with, no more lonely isolation, he would worship her for the goddess she was. Not even he could've made this happen.

"Fuck," she said, "Zee, if you don't stop, I'm going to make you build one of those dome places and keep you inside all day."

He chuckled. "Wouldn't get any disagreement from me."

She pushed him back, playful anger in her eyes. "Don't you think for a moment that I don't see what you're up to, young man."

Up to? He rubbed his hips against her and dipped down so the head of his cock poked at her opening, but with clothing blocking the way. She groaned and wiggled on him.

"Dammit," she said, "you're such a tease."

He tossed his head back and laughed. Goddess, his heart overflowed with light and happiness. Something he'd not felt in centuries. It was addictive and he wanted to keep it and her right here forever.

"Okay, back up, big boy. We're doing this."

His brows went up. Could he be so lucky? "Sex?"

She slapped his bare chest. "No," she sighed, "you're such a guy." She took his hand and tugged him behind her. "We're going to the village to see your sister and your people. You are their king, Zee. You have to act like one now. You're all grown up."

He lightly resisted. Just because he was grown didn't mean he knew how to lead. What if he made the wrong decision and more of his people died? He wouldn't be able to take it. They approached the backside of the sleeping domes.

"Zee, dammit," his mate said as she leaned forward, pulling with all her weight on his arm, "don't make me stop this car and come back there."

He hadn't realized he was offering so much resistance.

"Sorry," he said, quickly stepping forward, and watched as her eyes grew wide, and she fell with the sudden slack between them. "Oh dammit," he repeated her word and lifted her off the ground and onto her feet. He noticed she didn't have shoes. "We need to make you foot coverings. You could step on anything and become injured."

"Fine," she huffed, "we'll make them in the village."

He swallowed hard. "Yes, let's do that."

"It's *let's do this*," she corrected. He waved her forward not worried about messing up one of her human sayings.

They crossed between berms and emerged in the middle of the village with the fire and elders on one side and the food workstations on the other. Slowly, conversations quieted as more people stopped to stare at him.

Where the water jars stood, he saw his sister talking with Haml. He was probably informing her that he had returned. Oh, goddess. She was the queen, their alpha. What would she think about him taking all that away from her? She would hate him, want him to go. What about her people? No, he wasn't here to take back power.

As he eyed her, her face paled and her knees bent. Haml grabbed onto her to keep her from falling. Dammit, he knew this was a bad idea. She hated him so badly, she could take it. He turned toward the forest and stepped away. Fortunately, or unfortunately, his mate still held his hand, yanking him back.

"Yeah, I don't think so. Get your cute ass back here now."

He froze. Did she just say he had a cute ass, here in front of everyone? His face suddenly never felt as hot as it did that moment.

She laughed. "Come here." She wrapped her arms around him. "You can do this. You are the bravest man I know. How many people would've risked their lives to save me from a monster squid like you did?"

He ran his fingers along her jawline. "I would give my life for you, my mate."

Her eyes became glassy. Were those tears? Happy or sad? She laid her hand on his heart. "I can easily say I love you now. I know."

Unimaginable joy flowed through him. He

squeezed her to him, never wanting to let her go. "I've loved you from the moment I saw you."

"Then you can do this for me. Become who you were meant to be. I know how strong alphas are and how good they are to those they love. You deserve your own happy ending, Zee. I want that for you."

Somebody stopped behind his mate. He was almost too afraid to lift his eyes and see the anger and hate directed at him. But for her, he would.

He looked up and into eyes that were identical to his, a nose that was daintier, and lips like their mother's. "Iridia." Wren stepped to the side.

"Hello, little sister," he said. "You're all grown up. You look just like Mom." The mound of wall he had blocked all his emotions behind crumbled away. A sea of hurt, sorrow, grief, joy, and love hit him square in the heart. Never had he experienced so much at one time. It was overwhelming. This he did not expect.

Iridia stepped closer and hugged him. Shocked from her actions, he slowly put his arms around her. When he realized she didn't hate and want him gone, at this moment anyway, he hugged her too. He felt his sister's body-shaking sob and the tears on his chest.

He whispered to her, "I'm sorry I left you. I am so sorry I stayed away so long. I've missed you so much." As he said those words, they registered in his soul. Yes, he missed his parents, his sister, and best friend fiercely.

Never had he thought they would want him around. He was sure their hearts were closed to him. He had been wrong. There was only one person he could thank for this.

Iridia pulled back and turned. Everyone in the village had stopped what they were doing and had gathered around them. "All in the village," she shouted, "our king and alpha has returned."

Fear shot through his body. This was not what he had in mind.

CHAPTER TWENTY-THREE

"Iridia," he whispered, "I've not come back to take your place."

She swung around to face him, a frown and confusion on her face. "Then why are you here? Your people have missed you. They need a true leader."

He wanted to tell her he was not the person she thought he was. He was not a leader. He would not lead any others into death.

"We'll discuss this later," he whispered to her. "You are still the alpha."

She hit his arm exactly where Wren had last night. He cringed and rubbed the sore spot.

"No, I'm not," she whispered back. "You are the rightful heir." She poked his chest with a strong finger. He heard his mate giggle beside him. This was not funny.

"You are an heir also. You will remain the alpha," he answered.

His sister's lit up. "Is that an order from the alpha?"

"Yes," he growled, then immediately shook his head, "No." He wanted her to be the alpha. "I mean, yes, but no." Dammit.

Iridia winked and took his hand. "Everyone, continue with preparation for our meal. We have reason to rejoice and thank the goddess." Cheers went up and the camp became a bustle once again. Haml had joined them, a huge smile on his face. Xenos just didn't understand how they accepted him so readily.

"Come," Iridia said, "the elders would want to see you." She led them toward the fire on the far side of the village. From their slightly elevated position, they were able to see the entire community. Maybe that was why they sat there together instead of being part of the mass as they had been when his father ruled.

As they approached, the elder men stood. As he scanned their faces, the memories returned. Who they were and what part they played in the tribe.

They clasped arms, one at a time, until his reached the old storyteller.

"The prodigal son returns, I see," she said.

His brows drew down. "What?"

She cackled quietly. "It is a story for another place and time, child. Welcome back into the fold."

He bowed his head. "Thank you, Elder." Having greeted the group, he asked, "Why do you gather here instead of participating with the villagers?"

They each groaned, making his sister laugh. She even laughed like their mother had. The memory of his parents being killed would be forever at the fore of his mind with his sister as a constant reminder. But he was still glad he was here. He looked around for his mate and found her standing with her two friends by their berm.

"Alpha," one of the men said, "we are too old to do as the younger ones do, squatting to plant seeds or lifting metal to make knives. We are here for our knowledge only now as opposed to when your father was king."

Knowledge only? What kind of things did the village need that they hadn't already passed down through song and teaching?

Iridia held her hand out to him. "Let me show

you the rest of the village. It has changed a lot since you've been gone."

Pain and shame shot through him at her words. They were forced to change from losing so many tribal people. That was his fault. She sniffed the air then turned to gaze at him. What had she smelled? Did she sense the fear or dread he carried inside?

She gestured to the food stations as they passed by. "We still grow our own food in the honorable fashion. The older men with little to do have joined items to make new ones."

"Have they improved the broccola?" he asked, looking for the green tree-looking food.

"No," she replied, sticking out her tongue, "and I still won't eat it."

He laughed, and her shining smile lifted his soul. She was beautiful. "Who are you mated to? He is lucky."

Her smile fell. "I am not mated," she replied.

He stumbled to a stop. "Is your mate not among the villagers?"

She looked away. "We have decided that it would be better if I focus on the village as a leader instead of my own family as mother and mate."

Horror and grief stole through him. She couldn't

have a family because of him. Oh goddess, no wonder she wanted him to take over. He could not let his sister live being separated from her mate. He knew how she felt from being away from Wren just this morning. He would not wish such pain on his enemy.

He would become the alpha they expected of him.

"That isn't right, Iri. You should be able to have all you want."

A sad smile appeared on her face. "No matter what you choose in life, Xenos, there are sacrifices and consequences."

Oh, he understood consequences well. Familiar enough that he refused to make decisions. Already, he was questioning his decision to become the leader. How could he be a good ruler if he couldn't face the results?

"Iri," he asked, as he continued the walk through the village, "how do you know if you are making the right choices? Dad always did the right things. He never made mistakes."

A laughed burst from his sister. "Do you really believe that?"

He scrunched his brows. "Of course. He was perfect."

"Oh my goddess," she said, "you are much worse than even I thought. No wonder you ran."

Anger and shame once again shot through him. Anger winning. "You don't know—"

Her hands lifted in front of her. "Don't be angry, Xenos. No one is blaming you for anything." She sighed. "Let's sit for a moment." Off to the side, she raised two seats and sat on one. "Apparently," she started, "there's a lot about our parents you didn't see since you were out training to be the next alpha."

He couldn't argue with that. Along with Haml, his to-be-beta, he was busy learning all he could about everything during the day. At night, his father would sit with him to tell the young Xenos of decisions he'd made and why he figured what he did. His father was amazing in his logic and reasoning. His rule was always in the right.

"What did I not see?"

"How he made decisions for the tribe."

"I know why he made every call he did."

"No," she replied, "not 'why' but 'how.'"

"How what?" He didn't understand what she was trying to say.

"Xenos, Dad seldom made a decree without

discussing it with Mother and several of the elders."

He jerked to the side from shock so much that he nearly fell off the seat. Sure, he'd seen his father talking to many of the elders during the day, but he thought they were visiting like the alpha tried to do with everyone. His father grew up with the elders. He knew them well.

But during all those times, he was asking for advice? And Mom knew enough about village dealings that he spoke with her?

He got to his feet and paced. "I don't believe I didn't figure that out."

"Xenos, you idolized Dad. As did every young boy. In your eyes, he was a god that did no wrong. How could you have seen any flaws?"

"Is that why the elders sit by the fire? To discuss issues with you."

"Yes," she replied, "I got tired of having to track them down every time I wanted to talk with them."

Goddess, how could he have been so blinded? The solution to his problem was obvious. Another thought hit him.

"Iri, if Mom and Dad could make it as the alpha couple, there is no reason you and your mate can't. Especially if you have others to consult with. With

Haml as your beta, he can do anything you don't have time for. He doesn't have a mate, I don't think." He thought about the time he'd been spying and didn't remember any females around the beta.

He continued. "I've always wanted the best for you, Iri. Wanted you to be happy with your mate. And I still want that." He returned to his seat. As his mate said a short time ago, time to man up. He wrapped an arm around his sister's shoulders and pulled her against his side. Kissing the top of her head, he said, "I will release you from your duty to continue guiding the tribe. I will be the alpha I was supposed to be, *if* the tribe wants that. I'm not sure they do."

"Why would you think that?"

"Iridia," he said with a sigh. "The battle—"

"You don't know your own people, brother. Let them show you how they feel."

The call for the meal went out. "Let us eat and be joyful at your return." She stood with a smile and took his hand.

CHAPTER TWENTY-FOUR

Wren watched with her cousins, as Zee and Iridia walked away from the elders.

"What did we miss?" Lilah asked. "I thought he liked you."

Wren rolled her eyes. "He does like me. Iridia is his sister."

"No shit," Lilah said, "Hadn't seen that coming."

"So why is he a tiger roaming the jungles?" Daphne asked. "So, is he like the ruler now or is Iridia still in charge?"

That was a great question. Wren wasn't sure of the answer. He was so afraid of facing everyone that she couldn't imagine him readily saying yes to taking charge. She kept her eye on him and his sister as they made their way through the village.

"What's the plan for the day?" Daphne asked. "I'm starving."

"Yeah," Lilah said, "eating would be good. But then what?"

Wren chewed on her lip. "Well, I think it's rather obvious that we need to get to the island of the standing stones. With our rocks, a portal should open. Hopefully to the Crystal Kingdom if not Grandmom's."

"You think they are looking for us?" Daphne whispered.

"Of course, they are," Lilah replied. "There's got to be a million planets and shit in the universe, not to mention other dimensions, if those aren't in the same universe. I really have no idea how all that shit works."

Wren knew it was probably mind boggling when it came down to the truth of it all. Just accepting magic was hard enough.

"We need to talk with Iridia to see what she thinks. Maybe the storytelling lady will know more too. It would be great if this island was nearby."

"You know," Daphne said quietly, "if Zee is the king of this place, he will stay here."

Wren's heart crushed. The knowledge was there on the edge of her mind; she didn't want to consciously admit it. They had just told each other of their shared love. She was his mate. He said he'd be with her forever. That meant he was going with her or she was staying here.

She looked around the village that was like primitive camping at the national park. When she was a kid, camping was fun. But as she got older, and liked the modern conveniences, peeing behind a bush became a no go.

Could she suck it up and stay here with Zee? What did she have at home? Her writing, which she could do here with pen and paper brought over from Earth. Maybe she could teach those here how to write to put down their own stories for future generations. That would be so awesome. Now she was excited to stay and play teacher and historian.

Her mind was made up. She would do what she could to get the other two to the standing stones, but she'd stay with the man she loved.

A loud shriek whistled through the air, and the elders stood and headed toward the center of the village. There, tables had appeared from nowhere just like they had last night. Time for breakfast. She searched the crowd for Zee, seeing the little girl from yesterday first. The child came running for her.

"Wren, Wren. Sit with me." The girl was so adorable with her big eyes and long dark curls. How could she say no? She'd be with her mate the rest of the day.

Wren held her hand out. "Let's go. Show me where."

Two other young ones were aiming for Lilah and Daph. Seemed her friends had been adopted too. When everyone was seated, they joined hands, and the prayer of thanks to the Mother of the Land was said.

From where she sat in the middle of the tables, she could see Zee at the first table with Iridia and the elders. There was also a beautiful woman next to Iridia that Wren hadn't seen last night. The woman was stunning with a beautiful cocoa complexion, big eyes with a slight tilt for the perfect exotic look.

What made the woman stand out the most from the others was that she had breasts—about a size-A cup, but that was a lot more than any other female had. Fortunately, like Iridia, she wore many beaded necklaces and had long thick hair that covered most of her chest.

That was on thing Wren might not ever get used to. She wouldn't be giving up her sports bras and T-shirts for a long while. The villagers would just have to get used to it.

She caught Zee peeking at her, and she smiled at him. He winked and returned his attention to the elder speaking. Her heart melted. He was so perfect. So dreamy. Yes, she couldn't leave him; she was staying.

After most had finished eating, Iridia's friend got up and went into a mound. Her body was just a stunning as the rest of her. Wren wondered who her mate was. What a lucky guy.

One of the elders at the head table stood and called for quiet. Zee looked worried, his eyes remaining on his plate. The elder spoke of the days when the tribe was prosperous, before the qhasant came out of jealousy to take what they did not have.

Then he spoke of the brave males and females who fought and gave their lives in order for the gnoleon to win. There were great sacrifices. There always was when it came to survival. And without the courageous leadership of their young alpha, the gnoleon would have been enslaved and eventually wiped out as a race.

Wren could not have been prouder of her man than at that moment. She glanced at him to see him wide-eyed and staring at the elder. She shook her head at his modesty and humbleness.

The elder went on to explain the devastation of war on the souls of the survivors. The loss was beyond comprehension unless experienced. Many cold moons had passed, and the terrible toll on their new leader had been healed and now he had returned to bring back the glory that was the gnoleon race, created by the Mother of the Land to bring light to the darkness that wanted to rule. The elder asked Zee to stand.

Wren wiped her eyes with the collar of her shirt. Xenos stood with his shoulders back and chin held high. In his mind, he'd been forgiven and redeemed; his alpha persona had returned. He was gorgeous, and she was so happy he was hers.

The rest of the elders gathered around Zee, chanting or singing. With Zee in the middle of their circle, the group inched away from the table. One elder took the weapons off his back. Zee was about to snatch them back, a scowl on his face before another of the elders told him no.

Shiny liquid was poured onto his shoulders, and the older females rubbed the liquid down his arms, back and stomach. It was as if they were applying sunscreen on him for all day at the beach. All still chanting and moving away. Zee caught her eye, confusion filling his face. He had no idea what was going on.

Taking her eyes from the strange ceremony, Wren saw where they were headed. The same dome that the beautiful woman had gone into a short time ago.

She sat straight up, making sure what she was seeing was correct. In front of the mound opening, his loincloth was stripped from him, and he was pushed inside. The elders sealed the opening.

The old man that had been talking, turned back to the tables of the tribe members. "And now, the first duty of the reigning alpha shall be completed. Neither alpha nor mate are allowed to leave their home until an heir has been conceived. May the gnoleon live long." He raised his arm, and the people cheered.

Wren jumped to her feet, knocking her chair back. Everything in her turned cold and unfeeling.

That exquisite female had been chosen to be his mate. And he wouldn't be able to get out of the mating until the woman was pregnant.

Lilah's and Daphne's eyes were on her. Their shock was as apparent as hers felt. Wren felt sick, sweat breaking out on her forehead. She turned and hurried toward the mound she and Zee had shared.

She jerked her body in another direction. No, she couldn't go in there and see where they had been together only hours ago. Somewhere behind her, Haml called her name. She couldn't face him, couldn't face anyone. She broke into a run, cutting between mounds and into the woods.

CHAPTER TWENTY-FIVE

Wren ran through the woods with no place to go. She just kept running. Her heart was frozen and shattered into pieces. She cursed herself for being so gullible, so stupid, to fall in love with someone so perfect. She should've known someone like her, plain and boring, would never be allowed to have someone like Xenos.

But he had told her he loved her, that she was his true mate and would never leave her. Well, didn't take long for that to be proven a lie. In her stories, the alphas never lied to those they loved. They never hurt those who loved them in return.

And fucking-A, she wasn't writing one of her books. She was on a fucking alien planet controlled by evil, dark magic. What the fuck should she have expected? Evil was out to ruin all goodness and light. And it had done a perfect fucking job on her. All her happiness and light were dead. She wished she were too.

Tears blurred her vision, but she kept running. She wouldn't stop until her body was exhausted and couldn't go any longer. Maybe by then, she would've fallen off the edge of the planet into space where all the hurt would go away.

Her bare toes rammed into a root and she yelled, skidding on the ground. She grabbed her foot and cried, pulling into a ball of pathetic blubbering. She screamed out her anger into the forest around her. If she didn't let it free, she would've exploded.

Something soft touched her cheek. She opened her eyes to see leaves floating down from the trees above. They trees were crying with her, shedding the only thing they had to give. That's what she felt like—that she'd given all she had to him and she was bare. Exposed and naked with nothing to cover her leafless limbs.

The sunlight streamed through openings created by the sway of the sky-high canopy. The dust drifting among the beams sparkled like tiny fairy lights falling on and around her.

She tilted her head up to let the sun dry her tears. Taking a deep breath, she exhaled as much pain as she could. Not much remained now that she'd reach numbness. Except for her toe which still hurt like a motherfucker. Damn flip-flops.

Wren scooted toward a tree and leaned back against the sturdy base. On her drawn up knees, she laid her forehead. Her plans were changing once again. She was going with her cousins to the island of standing stones and porting away from this place.

"Well, what do we have here?"

Wren snapped her head up, hearing the grumbling voice. A few yards from her stood a half man/half something non-human. She stumbled to her feet and stepped back. A sting poked her ass and she brushed it away. When it happened on her other side, she glanced over her shoulder to see a three-foot-tall troll. Did trolls have long ears or long noses. Shit, she couldn't remember.

Wait. Kappy. These were called kappies. They'd seen one when they first arrived, and then one with the tiger/jaguar mama and cub. The two kappies behind her each had a spear naturally held at the level of her ass. She put her back to the tree again.

"Who are you and what do you want?" she asked the troll thing.

"Nothing you can't easily give me. I'm looking for a special gemstone," he said.

"I don't wear jewelry much." She splayed her fingers to show him. "I-I don't have anything you'd want to steal."

The troll leaned back and laughed. A deep, flehm sounding grunt and snorting. Maybe he was part pig. He grossed her out. And the little shits with spears freaked her out. It was like walking into a daycare center where all the three-year-olds were dressed up like Yoda with pointy wooden sticks instead of sabers.

"You look a lot like some friends of mine who live in the Crystal Kingdom."

That name caught her attention. "Do you have a way to get there?" If he knew of something, then maybe she could bribe him for the way.

"I certainly do." He stared at her with a twisted smile on his humanoid face.

"Awesome. If you tell me how, I'll see if I can get you some jewelry from the village."

"You don't understand, young lady." He stepped

closer to her. "To get back to the Crystal Kingdom, it takes a magic rock that only the Fairy Queen has shared."

"Oh." She realized what rock he was talking about. The one in her pocket. "I don't know the Fairy Queen. We were visiting my cousin with the elves."

He stepped closer, his smile becoming more sneering. "You may not, but you arrived here through a portal."

"What are you talking about?" Her instincts yelled for her to get the hell out of there. She glanced around at all the little shits surrounding her. She had no escape.

"Don't lie to me, human. I know who you are and where you came from. I want the stone." He held his hand out.

"It's at the village," she replied. "I don't carry it around with me."

His face twisted into a grimace with his eyes burning red. Her heart jumped, fear freezing her in place.

"Then we shall go to the village. We were on our way there anyway."

"Are you serious?" came out of her mouth before she could think about it. "They are going to eat your buddies for lunch. You know the real alpha has returned. The gnoleon are more powerful than they have ever been."

The troll/pig/human drew back. He seemed to be thinking. Did he know anything about Xenos? Apparently not if he believed her lie.

"I suggest you stay away from the village if you want to ever get back home. The alpha's beast is still on the edge and rather uncontrollable when angered. He'd rip your head off with one swipe then eat the rest of you."

The trolls eyes narrowed at her. She needed to shut off the verbal throw-up.

He pointed to his guards to come closer. "Perhaps, young lady, you can introduce us to the alpha. Then you can fetch your stone for me, and we'll be gone."

Her intuition balked at the idea of giving this creature a way into the kingdom where her family was. But the spear points too close to her vital organs had her rethinking things.

There was another option of escaping that she would've never considered before yesterday. She placed her hands flat against the tree. *Anything you can do to help me get away from these evil creatures would be great.* She waited but nothing happened. So much for magic over trees.

Troll guy gestured to his dwarfs. "Push her that way."

She hurried forward before they had a chance to draw blood. She had no doubt that would've made them happy. As she stepped out from the trunk, little shits behind her, the wind in the trees picked up. At least, that's what it seemed like.

Wren glanced up to see to see two limbs bending toward the ground. She threw her arms up for something to grab onto and she found herself flying up through the air as the guards were swept away like dirt under a rug. Another stem wrapped around her waist and took her higher into the tree well out of their reach.

The troll stood opened mouth, staring up at her. Then he smirked. "All right. I guess we'll see you and the villagers as they run out of the woods to the creek. And as they do, we will kill each and every one, including the children, until I get my stone."

She snorted. Whatever. There was no reason why they would leave the protection of the forest. And if they tried to invade the village, the little guys would never make it over the high domes creating a barrier around the living area. She wasn't worried until she saw troll guy use magic to create a fireball between his hands.

The fire snapped and crackled differently than normal fire. The flames were a deeper red, some almost black. The reason hit her—black magic. The troll was using black magic to start a forest fire to chase everyone to the creek for safety. Holy shit. She had to do something. As she watched, troll dickhead threw the ball into the tree next to her. Almost instantly, the entire tree was ablaze with the fire stretching out to other trees and grabbing on.

This was so not good.

CHAPTER TWENTY-SIX

Xenos could not believe the elders had taken his clothing and shoved him into a berm, then sealed the door. What the dragon shit were they trying to do? Then he heard movement behind him and smelled female arousal.

As soon as the scent hit him, his tigron cringed, because it smelled sour compared to their mate's. It did not want this female inside with him. He spun around to see a beautiful female with breasts larger than any female in the village, except his mate.

"Hello, Alpha." Her voice was soft and creamy. She strode up to him, placing her hand on his chest, sliding it down his stomach, below his waist. When he snapped out of his stupor, realizing now what the plan was, he thrust his hips back before her hand reached his cock.

"I apologize," he said. With him bent over with his ass sticking back, she leaned forward and placed her lips on his. He snapped back so quickly that he hit his head against the entrance wall that had been sealed.

He scooted around to the side, trying to avoid her hands. She seemed to have four of them as he was having difficulty fighting her off. "No, really," he said. "I can't do this."

She smiled at him. "Don't worry about that, My King. I am the chosen one for you. I've been preparing for your return. I will get you able to do this.'"

"That's what I'm afraid of," he mumbled, pulling her hand away from his cock again. "I don't want to make anyone mad, but—"

The female suddenly took her hands back. "Am I not pretty enough for you?" Tears filled her eyes and now he felt like dragon shit for upsetting her.

"You are beautiful, truly—" Her smile returned as did her hands. He was sure his ass was smeared with dirt from dragging it along the wall trying to escape her lithe fingers. "No, you don't understand—"

"I do, My King. Just relax and let me do what I've been trained to do."

He finally grabbed both her hands in his. "That's the problem. I don't want you to do something because it's your duty. You need to *want* to do it because you love the one you're with."

She stared at him. "I don't understand. The king must have an heir immediately. That is tradition."

Was that so? "Then why doesn't my sister have a child? She was the leader for two hundred cold moons."

"She does have a child."

He froze in place. Had he not heard his sister tell him she had a child when she mentioned that she and her mate decided not to be together so she could focus on leading? Had he missed that? "But she doesn't have a mate," he finally said.

"She is as stubborn as you seem to be," she said. "Iridia refuses to mate because she's afraid her family will become to ingrained with their leadership duties in the tribe. And if you returned, they would lose all they had done and worked for in the village. She doesn't want them to feel unwanted."

"That's not a good reason for denying herself a

family. What is wrong with her? Mom taught her better than that."

"I do not know, My King. I was not given that information."

"Please, call me Xenos. That is my name."

"Only a mate may call you by your name. And I will do as you wish."

"No, wait," he said. How could he forget all the rules to being an alpha? He'd had them drilled into his head for three hundred cold moons. Her eyes began to tear up again. Dragon shit.

"What is your name?" he asked.

"Nova, daughter of Traig."

"Nova, is there a male in the village that is your mate?"

Her chin dropped to her chest. "I am the one chosen for you. I can have no other mate."

Hope filled his mind. "So you do have a mate. Someone you love with your heart. Someone you want to be with all the time." She tilted her head to the right. He had to be careful with his words. "Nova, I found my true mate and I love her."

"The elders," she whispered, "they will not accept the strange female as your mate. You must mate in the gnoleon line."

"I refuse to turn my back on her. I'll love her forever."

Nova looked up at him. "Then you must give up your alpha position so your sister may resume her leadership."

"And she gives up her family if she rules." Xenos stepped away from her, a growl in his throat. The female gasped and scampered to the far side. "I am sorry. My animal is. . .not happy at the moment. I need to go."

"The elders have sealed the entrance with a strong magic. We are not to leave until I am with child."

"They will learn. No one keeps me from being who I am or going where I wish." He shifted into his tigron and began digging at the ground in front of where the exit should be. In a matter of moments, his large paws had scooped out mounds of dirt that allowed him to go under the dome wall to the other side.

He emerged in his tigron form daring any elder to tell him to go back inside. Everyone in the vicinity backed off as he bared his teeth. He needed to find his mate. He had to talk with her to make a decision as to whose heart he was going to break— either his sister's or his mate's.

He sniffed the air, scenting for a recent trail. He caught nothing. Haml burst through the crowd outside the dome. "She ran into the forest, Xenos. She saw you go inside with the female, and she left." He pointed. "She went that way." With two bounds, he was outside the village's perimeter, following the fragrance of his upset and sad mate.

What was he going to do? Who was he going to deny having a family? One of the two females he loved would have a ruined life because of him. Once again, he had to make a decision that would end in disaster for someone. How could he choose?

His animal's nose picked up a strange smell. It was familiar, yet it wasn't. Did someone have a cooking fire out here? Why would they? It would be much easier to bring the food to the village to cook over the pits.

He quickened his pace. Something was wrong. His tigron felt fear, which seldom happened. He heard thrashing ahead and a familiar scream with curse words he was learning. His mate!

Dashing forward, he saw her hopping on one leg as she held her foot in her hand. He shifted before reaching her.

"Zee," she nearly cried.

He took her into his arms and lifted her off the ground, planting kissing all over her face. "Why did you run?" he asked between pecks.

"Really? You have to ask?" She was breathing so hard, he was afraid she'd go into one of her attacks. "I saw you go into a dome, naked, with a women I can't begin to compare to. The stunning face, her beautiful hair, perfect body." She choked on sobs.

He set her down, cupping her face in is hands. "Wren, you are my love, my mate. I don't want to be with anyone else." He'd never want anyone else, but that may not matter in the future. "She doesn't begin to compare with you. You are perfect to me." His thumb brushed away a tear.

"Really? You mean that?" she asked.

He drew her close and kissed her, putting everything he felt into the kiss in case it was their last.

She pushed him back. "Hold that thought. We have to get everyone out of the woods. There's a fire coming."

He lifted his nose, the burning smell was stronger. "How was a fire started? There should not have been anyone out here."

"It was this half troll/half human thing with a

hundred of those little shits the mama tigers chased."

"Kappies?"

"With spears. They were downright scary. Like fugly toy clowns come to life."

He wasn't sure what she just said, but he recognized the words *weapons* and *fear*. He took her hand and headed toward the village.

"The troll threw a ball of fire into the trees after a tree saved me from them. The fire is moving faster than possible. It's like it's on a rampage to burn everything."

He stopped. "Black fire?"

Her eyes were wide with fright. "I saw black streaks in the fire. Evil magic, right?"

"Yes, magic with a mission to kill everything in its path. We have to move faster. Get on my back." He shifted into his tigron and lay on the ground for her to get on.

"Oh shit," she griped as she threw a leg over his back, "are you sure about this? I've never even ridden a horse before."

This won't be any horse ride, my love. He couldn't tell her that in this form, but she'd figure that out in a moment. With his first step, she rocked backward, legs flying up, but she grabbed a fistful of his fur and pulled herself down, wrapping arms around his neck. When she was settled, he kicked it up a notch, and she screamed another curse into his neck as he ran full out.

At least the decision for this was easy. They all had to get to the creek and on the other side. There was too much of a gap for even black fire to jump. They would be safe.

Reaching the village, he roared to get everyone's attention. He hoped the older ones remembered his father was also a tigron, even though he seldom changed forms. He padded up to Iridia standing with the elders and sat so his mate could stand. She slid off his back, landing on her ass on the ground and lay with a deep sigh.

"We are never doing that again," she said. Iridia helped her up as he changed.

"We need to move quickly," he said. "Black fire is eating the forest."

Those nearby gasped. "From where? Who would start it?"

Xenos frowned. "I've felt and seen strange things lately. The dark magic is somehow gaining strength. My mate has seen a creature I do not know of. It has the ability to make the black magic."

One of the elders stood. "We must get to the creek."

"No," his mate blurted. "These evil creatures said they will be waiting there to kill everyone. We can't go there."

"That's the only place to go to escape such magic," another elder said.

"What about the jungle?" Wren asked.

"It is beyond the creek."

"Shit," his mate grumbled.

"What would you like to do, Alpha?" Iridia asked.

He looked around at those staring at him. "No matter what, we're leaving. Have everyone start packing only the necessities. Gather the children." He grabbed his sister's arm. "Including your own," he finished with a frown. He would discuss her choice to not inform him of all the truth later.

"Zee," Wren said, "you *cannot* go to the creek. They are waiting to kill all of you."

Fear shot through him. "What other choice do we have?" At that moment, he watched as the cleared tables from the meal slid under the dirt where they were kept until the next meal.

"Oh," Wren said, "that's so cool. I wondered where they were kept. Wait," she turned to him, "can everyone just wait out the fire in their domed homes? Fire can't burn the dirt, right?"

"Black fire does," one of the elder said. "It penetrates the ground to destroy even the magic in the soil."

He liked her idea of going underground. With a normal fire, that would've been the solution. "How far down does it burn? What if we dig a hole. . ." No, that wouldn't work. His people couldn't breathe in dirt, just move it.

They needed a way to get to the other side of the creek without being seen. His eyes roamed the area as he thought, glancing at the hole he had dug to get under the dome wall earlier to get out.

"That's the answer," he said. "We dig a tunnel under the creek and come up far behind the kappies."

An elder scoffed. "That would take much too long, even with our magic."

"Maybe with magic," he said, "but not with my tigron."

"That might work," the storyteller replied, coming forward. "Use your magic to push the dirt down and to the side as well as digging back. That will leave less soil to crawl through."

He hadn't thought about that. As he dug, the

dirt would've piled up behind him. But by compacting it around them, it was out of the way as well as made the tunnel stronger.

"How close can you get to the creek before the kappies see you?" Wren asked. "You can get started there, and we'll make sure everyone starts that way."

"We hadn't thought of that, young human," an elder said. "Yes, take the path halfway then dig. Now go."

Xenos took her hand to go with him, but she pulled back. "I need to help the village pack. Take the elders with you since they may take the longest to get through." She grimaced and turned to the older people. "Sorry," she said.

"It is the truth. Don't be sorry for how things are," the storyteller said to her. "Let's go."

Xenos hugged her close and kissed her. This would not be his last kiss. They would survive this.

"Go," Wren pushed on his chest, "I'll see you there."

He held her in front of her, staring into her eyes. "I love you," he said sternly, making sure she understood.

She smiled. "I love you to, *my* mate. Now get some clothes then get going."

He forgot that he was completely nude still.

"Here." Haml threw him their skimpy outfit. Xenos caught it and ran off along the path. He had a lot to do in a short amount of time, but his tigron could do it. Hopefully.

CHAPTER TWENTY-SEVEN

Wren watched as Zee left to do his thing. Looking around the village at all the running people, she swallowed hard. There were so many things to do. Pack personal belongings, get the dishes, the water jugs, find the children, what about food? Are all those needing help getting it?

Her pulse jumped with her mind crowding with so many things. Her breathing shallowed and quickened. Not now! This was not time for a panic attack. What had Zee told her earlier?

Pick the most important thing and do that first, pushing away all else. Okay, she could do that. She needed to find her cousins. Shit, she'd totally forgotten about them.

Wren found Lilah and Daphne and dragged them to the side. "Hey, guys," she said, "we've got a problem."

"What?" they asked.

"Do you both have your stones with you?" Her cousins patted their pockets and both nodded. "Good. Now listen. There is some half human-looking thing that wants one of our stones so he can open a port to the Crystal Kingdom."

"He knows how to get back? Let's go with him," Daph whispered.

"I didn't get the feeling he wants to go for a vacation. He was prepared to kill me to take mine. I told him it was here in the village. He's the one who started the fire we're running from."

"Shit," Lilah said, "that's all we need. Someone hunting us. Fuck. What are we going to do?"

"Right now, we're loading up with the villagers and moving through the tunnel. Help who you can and get going."

All right, that task was done. What was next most important? The children.

Iridia and a couple others had the kids in a line, each carrying a bag with their possessions. Several had dirt smears on their faces where tears were falling. But the alpha leader was hugging and talking to each, comforting them. She looked to be a natural mother.

Wren noticed the smell of smoke and glanced out into the woods. In the near distance, she saw flashes of red.

"Hurry, it's coming," she yelled. "Get to the path and the tunnel now."

The children were off with several adults guiding them. She had no idea there were so many. Their village would soon be large again.

She glanced around, searching for anyone struggling. Seeing none, she started checking the domes to make sure no one was left inside or needed help. By the time she made it around, most of the village was gone and the air was heavy with smoke. She coughed, fanning the air in front of her face.

Iridia and a few men were left. The tops of the mounds were burning on the back side of the perimeter.

"Come on, Iridia, let's go. Get the men going."

With sad eyes, the alpha glanced one last time at her and her people's home. Wren had no doubt they would rebuild bigger and better. Her coughing became worse. Iridia called for everyone to leave and Wren led them down the path.

The fire was literally nipping at their heels. At the entrance to the tunnel, she directed the guys inside. Iridia made her go first, and she wasn't about to argue. She dropped to her knees and started crawling.

Iridia called behind her. "We need to get you shoes."

Wren laughed. "Sure, why not?" As she crawled, she noted the small glowing things that Zee had called up through the ground in their dome last night so it wasn't pitch dark. She knew earth had creatures in the oceans that glowed, giving off light, but she wasn't sure about the ground. But they sure came in handy at the moment.

Behind her, Iridia cried out. "What's wrong?" Wren hollered.

"The fire is burning into the tunnel. It is following the dirt." The alpha coughed.

"Oh shit," she whispered. Nobody had thought of that. They needed to seal off the end. The tunnel wasn't wide enough to move around. One direction was it. "Iridia," Wren said, "make the tunnel fill in behind you. Pull the dirt down."

"It's not enough. The fire is eating through it."

"Shit." Okay, now what? They needed a large amount of dirt all at once to choke the air from the tunnel. "Iridia, I need to crawl as fast as you can until I say stop, okay?"

"Yes, go!"

Wren pounded her knees and hands into the hard dirt as they raced forward. Wren closed her eyes and asked the trees above them to push the ground to close the tunnel. For their roots to dig in and collapse the gap so the fire couldn't follow. And to please try not to bury them alive.

She crawled what felt like hours. The pain in her knees was slight compared to what she would've thought they'd be by now. When the ground started to slant down, the composition of the dirt became rocky and damp. In her mind, she imagined crossing under the creek. Even though it wasn't logical, she felt like she had to be as quiet as possible to not be heard by the soldiers above land.

After being with the friendly gnoleon people, coming across the armed group seemed weird. There was no question they meant to take whatever they wanted by force if necessary. What they wanted, Wren and her cousins refused to give up. Whatever reason the leader wanted the stones couldn't have been good. That in itself was reason enough to keep him from getting what came for.

Hopefully after this, she'd never have to see

their ugly mugs again. They stirred a bad feeling inside her.

About the time she was going to call a break, her eyes noticed light ahead. Continuing to move forward, she approached the end, and Zee reached in and nearly dragged her out then squeezed her in his arms. She didn't know why he was worried.

"We're okay," she said. "Iridia and I are the last ones."

He nodded and pressed her lips together. Yeah, she got it as she smiled around his fingers. They had to be quiet in case the armed little shits could hear them. She wondered how far away they were. She crawled forever after passing the creek.

Haml helped Iridia to the surface, ending the successful escape attempt. Together, the four led the tribe through the forest coming to the jungle. During the flee, she noted Iridia and Haml held hands while she carried a child on her hip. Boy, she hadn't seen that coming. But who would be the logical counterpart to a female born of an alpha? If not another alpha, then certainly a beta.

At the edge of the forest, a few yards from the giant jungle plants, Zee called a halt and the group began setting up camp. They were hours away from the creek, and Zee didn't seem worried about being followed.

Wren watched as men and women used their magic to lift the dirt into hollowed domes. Those carrying leather bags moved belongings into the arched ground, children coming out with large bowls and containers she'd seen when the village was preparing to eat.

They had trailed the creek the entire way, which made gathering water much easier than in the previous location. The swift moving creek had grown into a wide slow-moving river.

Children and adults returned with berries and apples, the same as what she and her cousins ate on their way to the tribe. The gardens they had were left behind. No doubt burned to a crisp.

Wren realized the dinner tables in the village wouldn't be here. Nobody had brought the tables along, obviously. They would have to eat on the ground. She thought back to the time with Avery in the CrystalKingdom, and how the elves used the tree limbs and roots to create tables and chairs. Could she do the same?

Zee had told her she had magic ability to control the trees, which the gnoleon couldn't do. She could believe the connection considering how the forests comforted her when young. She spent a lot of time climbing and sitting among trees. But magic?

She'd never done anything strange with "magic powers" on Earth. But, then again, she wasn't on her home planet anymore. How would she know if she didn't try?

Wren looked around and saw everybody busy doing something, except for her and her two cousins. "Hey," she said to her friends, "go find some way to help." To their credit, they jumped in and helped with food prep. She slowly shuffled to the closest tree and leaned against it nonchalantly.

Letting out a deep breath, she placed both hands on the smooth trunk. Well, if she had magic, now was the time to show it. In her mind, eyes closed, she replayed the meal gathering in the elven villages.

The palm of her hands tingled, but she didn't feel the tree move to lower branches or lift roots. Zee and Haml were wrong. She was just a plain human from a non-magical world.

Her mate must've noticed what she was doing. Just as she was about to give up, his warm familiar body pressed against her back, hot hands covering hers against the bark to keep her in place. She felt as if her heart was being pulled from her chest.

No, that wasn't right. She wasn't being pulled, her heart was pushing, spilling out an invisible force she'd never experienced. How had all that been locked inside her? The feeling was beyond words even for a wordsmith like her. How about a Niagra Falls of emotions and. . .power?

Her legs wobbled and shook, didn't feel as if they could support her anymore. Her arms became impossibly heavy, her forehead falling against the tree. Suddenly, she was weightless and floating through the air. No. That wasn't right either. Zee's scent surrounded her. He was carrying her. Why was that?

Then warm softness enveloped her, taking her down into sleep.

CHAPTER TWENTY-EIGHT

During the next two days of travel through the jungle, Wren had remained at Zee's side, as he led them safely along a trail he'd discovered in his isolation.

Nobody, including Zee, had said anything about what happened when she tried to use her magic. After passing out, she slept through until the next morning. With the rush to get on the road, or trail as it were, she didn't get to ask him what the result had been. Had she made a fool of herself?

Since her attempt at using magic, the air around the villagers had changed. Before they had been welcoming and friendly but always kept their distance. Now she felt as if they wanted to include her. What had changed and why?

On top of that, old worry stirred in her. Would she and Zee remain together? He was the alpha of a village. They needed him. She didn't belong in this world. She was the alien the tribe had been nice enough to take in. But they had made it clear that she wasn't welcome as the mate of their leader.

Without slowing, Zee sniffed, then gave her a concerned expression. "What is wrong? I scent your concern."

She frowned. "That nose is not fair. If I can't smell you, you can't smell me."

"I agree," he said, "I will stop breathing for you."

She thumped him on the bicep with a flick of her finger off her thumb. "Don't be a smart ass."

He chuckled lightly then went quiet, waiting on her to answer. She sighed, looking around to see how close the others were. "I just don't know what's going to happen with us."

He abruptly stopped. "I don't understand. We will be together until it is our time to join those who have passed before us." The line of people behind them groaned as, like a row of dominoes, they ran into the back of the person ahead of them.

Wren swallowed her negative emotions for the moment. This wasn't the time or place to make such big decisions. Besides, the facts were clear. The elders wanted Zee, and she wanted to go home.

Zee called for a midday break. She took the opportunity to ask him more questions. She pulled him aside. "Zee," she started, "Why hasn't the woman picked out to be your mate tried to take my place with you?"

He smiled. "Because she's not my mate. You are." He hugged her to him.

"Yeah, but that didn't stop the elders before."

His body jiggled with laughter. "You used your magic, love."

Lilah and Daph had told her how the tables spontaneously grew from the roots out of the ground and how amazed everyone was. The two also asked why she didn't eat. They hadn't realized that Wren had created it all. She wasn't sure she had.

She said, "What has that got to do with anything? And what happened there? Why did I pass out?"

Zee pulled her onto his lap as he sat on a boulder along the bankside of the river. "Wren, our people's magic is tied to the land." She didn't miss the pronoun he used. He was including her. "The gnoleon fae get their abilities from sharing energies with the plants and life around them."

"How do they do that? Share."

"Well, that's hard to explain," he replied. "When I use magic, I talk in my mind to ask the dirt to do what I need. Then the magic in my heart joins with the ground's magic to do what I asked."

"Your heart?" Wren asked. She thought back to that moment with the tree. She'd felt as if her chest was being pulled out of her, then she realized that sensation wasn't correct. She was pushing out. Was it her magic going into the tree as her part of the sharing?

Zee repositioned her on his lap. He was getting hard under her ass. A thrill rushed through her knowing she had that effect on him.

He cleared his throat. "Magic comes from the heart, love." His hand rested above her left breast, his pinky finger rubbing over the swell of her boob. She grabbed his wandering digits, looking around to see if anyone noticed. He just chuckled. Men.

"I didn't feel that sharing of my heart until you

came up behind me and placed your hands on mine. Why?"

"I didn't think at that time that you'd consciously used your magic before according to how you reacted when I mentioned it earlier. My sister told me how the tunnel from the old village collapsed to keep the fire from entering, but I don't think she knew how it really occurred. I suspect your magic played a part."

She nodded. She had asked the tree roots to help stop the fire, but she didn't know if the flames were extinguished or if she and Iridia had just crawled away fast enough. She didn't feel then like she did standing at the tree to make tables. Her hands just tingled until Zee joined her.

She said, "When your touch combined with mine, that's when I felt this overwhelming feeling pouring from my chest."

"My magic was showing yours how to work itself. That's when all the tree roots in the area exploded out of the ground and formed into tables."

She turned to him. "That really happened? I mean, that was my goal, but I don't remember seeing anything."

"Love," he said, "you had an incredible amount

of magic coming out of you. I think you let everything you had go into creating that moment. There
were tables as far as we could see. I need to show
you how to control the exchange so you don't
completely drain yourself like you did. You were
so exhausted, I don't think you could open your
eyes."

Ah, that made sense. A smile inched across her
face.

She really had magic. Tree magic.

For the rest of that second day, Zee spent time
walking and speaking with various elders, while
Iridia and Haml continued leading the group along
the trail through the jungle. Zee asked her to stay
with Iridia at the head of the villagers. She
wondered what he was doing, but she was sure it
was alpha business. Huge changes were upon
them.

As the shadows on the ground grew longer, the
flora began to change from tropical leafy, to grassy
open fields, then forest. Zee called out to set up
camp, and the villagers scattered to do their duties.

With Zee's help, Wren once again worked her
magic. This time, everyone including her cousins
were present and witnessed her abilities.

When the meal came to an end, the storyteller

elder stood from her place at the tables, gaining the attention of the crowd.

"On behalf of the alpha and elders, I will create the story of our great exodus that will become part of our history to pass down through our children. We will remember the destruction of the land and the rise of the dark magic. We will remember the return of our alpha who went away in order to discover our new home. And himself.

"The story of the arrival of the three from our goddess's land to remind us that, when in a strange world, it is important to accept what we cannot control and to not lose ourselves among fear of change."

Wren startled on her seat of dirt. She realized that in all that had happened in the last few days, nothing had sent her spiraling into an attack. Just about everything that had happened to her had been out of her control. All except how she handled the evacuation efforts with calm completion of individual tasks.

She turned to her mate sitting beside her and smiled at him. He'd been the reason she was able to overcome and accept what she could and couldn't control. With him by her side, she would grow into the strong woman she'd always wanted to be.

That thought reminded her of the biggest issue still lingering between her and Zee. Who would say goodbye to their home and family?

Her heart said there was no problem here. As did her brain—they had to return home, and Zee was not a part of her world no matter how much she wanted him to be. The elders had been right to make Zee's mate someone from the tribe, someone from his own world.

The female elder called her name, snapping her from her thoughts. She watched as Iridia's council gathered at the head of the table. What was happening? What had she missed? Zee squeezed her hand and smiled at her. His eyes twinkled. Oh, that worried her. The last time she saw that look, a shirt-pouch full of berries were crushed between them.

When the elders had formed a half circle, Zee pulled her from the table to stand before the older group.

"Wren of planet Earth," one of the men said, "we apologize for our attempt to keep you from joining with our alpha. We did not know you carried the magic of the female alpha mate. You were wise to keep it secret from strangers who would use that power to allow the dark magic to rise."

She raised a brow to Zee. What the hell were they talking about? She didn't intentionally hide anything. He just winked. Oh god, no telling what he told the elders about her. But he knew long before she did what was inside her.

The elder man took her hand and Zee's and placed them on top of each other. Another of the older ones wrapped a leather cord around their wrists binding them together. She swallowed hard. Was this what she thought?

The man raised his arms. "Our alpha has chosen his mate wisely, and their mating has already begun."

A gush of horror raced through her. Did the man just tell the whole village that she and Zee were having sex? Oh god! She could never look at them all again.

"All that remains to make Wren of Earth the alpha female is acknowledgement from the tribe." Zee turned her to face them. Well, shit. So much for never looking at them again. He lifted their tied hands overhead.

Then those at the tables did the same. Couples held up clasped hands and singles lifted one arm.

"It is unanimous," the elder called out, "Wren, alpha female, your people welcome you."

"Oh my god, Wren," Lilah yelled-whispered, "I think you just got married."

Wren gasped, agreeing with her cousin. Joy filled her, tears forming. The man of her dreams, and stories, was hers. She'd always dreamed of getting married as the sun set fire to the sky with all colors of the rainbow lighting the earth. She hadn't planned on wearing an old T-shirt and shorts, though. Eh, at least planning the ceremony was easy.

The elders returned to the table, unwrapping her hand from Zee's. He didn't move even though she was more than eager to sit and get out of the spotlight.

Zee raised his hands, drawing the villagers' attention. "Friends, I'd like to thank everyone for their hard work and patience on this journey to a new home. In consultation with the elders and Iridia, I have decided that this location will be our new home. There is much we have to do, but I think we will be better and stronger than before."

The tribe cheered and slapped their hands on their thighs. That must've been their way of applauding. She had so much to learn about them.

Wait. Was that her decision? To say goodbye to her family and friends to stay with him. Her heart told her yes. She would give up everything to be by the side of her mate.

"Also, soon our friends from the Crystal Kingdom will start their journey to the Island of the Standing Stones in their desire to return to their home."

Whoa. What was he about to declare? The way he spoke, it seemed like he meant for her to leave with her cousins. He wanted her to go? After they were just wed?

Zee continued. "As you all know, Wren is my alpha mate. She is the one who gave me the strength to see how wrong I was to be away from those I love. She made me realize that with her by my side, I would always have someone to share my thoughts, ideas, and dreams."

He glanced at Iridia who sat next to Haml holding his hand. She smiled at her brother. "After talking with the elders and my family, I have made the decision that I will be accompanying my mate on her trek."

Wren gasped and slapped her hands over her gaping mouth. Tears of happiness filled her eyes.

"I have complete faith that my sister, Iridia, will

continue to lead you as she has for many cold moons. She's probably done a better a job than I would have." He nodded toward her. "And now with her mate at her side, as a mate and beta, I'm certain they will be even better."

He scooped her into his arms. "Now, we're off to continue our mating."

Her jaw dropped as she squeezed his lips together. "Don't tell them that. I can't believe you said that." She hid her face against his chest and laughter trailed them.

CHAPTER TWENTY-NINE

Wren was mortified but eager for their next round of mating. Zee walked into a dirt hut and laid her on a pallet of blankets that were spread out. Then she was on her back on the bed with Zee pressed to her body. He cupped her face, rocking his hips into the juncture of her thighs.

He nibbled her lips, sucking, and licking, and trailing his tongue down her neck to the valley of her breasts. Then he took a hardened nipple into his mouth and sent electricity shooting to her clit. Every suck felt like a new shockwave of fire jetting through her body.

"Oh, Zee," she mumbled, her throat dry as sandpaper as she raked her nails through his hair.

She gripped the strands and pushed her breast further into his mouth. "That feels so good."

She squealed at the feel of his hands roaming up her thigh to the waistband of her clothing, he quickly undressed her.

He slid a hand over her satin covered crotch, and she moaned.

She gasped the moment his lips brushed over her clit through her underwear. Zee looked up and grinned, then pulled her underwear down and tossed them over his shoulder. He leaned down and blew hot air on to her clit. Then wrapped his arms under her body to hold her in place.

"Oh, my…"

She tightened her hold on his hair, tugging his strands and lifting her ass closer to his face involuntarily. He did a slow circle over her clit with his tongue, dancing it over her entrance, to her aching pleasure center. A low, raspy moan left her throat. He licked up and down her clit with sure strokes that had her groaning for more.

Heat expanded in her belly to the point she thought she'd internally combust. Her muscles tightened and before she got a chance to take a breath, the tension in her belly snapped so fast it left her gasping. Her back arched off the bed. Her legs clenched around his head and everything, but the amazing feeling rushing through her, was forgotten.

Then he was there again, the head of his cock rubbing at her swollen folds, pushing into her aching pussy.

He drove deep, filling her in a single-minded thrust. There was no stopping. He pulled back and did it again. With every drive into her, he pushed her further up the bed, and the hands around her hips rammed her right back toward his dick. There were no words to describe how he felt inside her. It was an overwhelming sense of being filled to the brim.

Zee grunted.

She could only hold on, whimper and feel her heart ready to burst with each breath she took.

He slipped a hand around her thigh and pressed at her clit with his fingers. She saw stars. He gripped her left hip hard with his other hand. "Let yourself go. Take me with you."

The world narrowed to only their harsh breathing and the sound of skin slapping. Explosions rocked her as waves of pleasure consumed her from head to toe. She clung to the bed, her body shivering, and her pussy grasping tightly at his cock.

With every breath came another shudder and mini aftershock and then he plunged into her one final time, held still and grunted loudly as he filled her with his seed.

EPILOGUE

Wren, her mate, and her two cousins were ready to leave for the Island of the Standing Stones. The new tribal home had been set up, and the garden had been started in the fields. Various members of the tribe whittled and cut wood to recreate their tsbles, and water barrels, and necessities left behind.

A rough map had been put together with the knowledge of the elders, legends, and what Xenos knew from his travels. She didn't know how well the map would work, but it was all they had.

Loaded with packs of food and water, and for Wren a new pair of shoes identical to Zee's, the four were off. Thanks to the village's new location, they were closer to the mountain range that presented their first challenge to cross.

Soon after leaving, the land sloped at a low incline reminding Wren of the torture devices called a stair stepper exercise machine.

"Ugh," Lilah said behind her. "Isn't there a different way to get to this place. I hate hiking uphill."

"This will pass quickly," Wren said. "We'll be over the top in a few hours. Then it's easy going."

"I can't wait," her cousin said.

Reaching the level on the mountainside where the trees stopped growing, the group paused and looked over the forest behind them. The beauty was breathtaking until Wren saw the distinct break between green leafy foliage and black, burned land. Her heart sank at the devastation.

Zee squeezed her hand. "In time, the land will heal. The dark magic of the planet has never been completely in control."

"I remember the woman telling us about the evil magic creating this planet. But what did the guy who married us mean by the *rise of the dark magic?*"

"I've felt the change too," he replied. "Something or someone has been claimed by the evil force embedded in our existence. The creature that attacked you in the creek, I hadn't ever seen. But the elders spoke about beasts like those. They had been banished for the longest time while the peaceful fae controlled the dimension.

"But with this new entity, the dark magic once again has a vehicle in which to administer its power. Those elements connected with the black magic are reappearing, gaining strength."

"Is there anything we can do to stop it?" Daphne asked. "Wren said the creatures that cornered her in the trees wanted our portal stones. Why would they want that?"

"Besides the obvious, I don't know," Zee replied.

Wren hoped that when they got home in a few days, Grandmom would know what to do. Before she killed all three of them for screwing up with her stones.

Soon. They'd find a way to get everyone home. Well, everyone else. She was staying with Zee. She'd never felt so much a part of a community like she did his people. But her cousins needed to get home, and she'd do whatever necessary to help them find their way back.

The End...for now.

ABOUT THE AUTHOR

New York Times and USA Today Bestselling Author

Hi! I'm Milly Taiden. I love to write sexy stories featuring fun, sassy heroines with curves and growly alpha males with fur. My books are a great way to satisfy your craving for paranormal romance with action, humor, suspense and happily ever afters.

I live in Florida with my hubby, our kids, and our fur babies: Speedy, Stormy and Teddy. I have a serious addiction to chocolate and cake.

I love to meet new readers, so come sign up for my newsletter and check out my Facebook page. We always have lots of fun stuff going on there.

SIGN UP FOR MILLY'S NEWSLETTER FOR LATEST NEWS!

http://eepurl.com/pt9q1

Find out more about Milly here:
www.millytaiden.com
milly@millytaiden.com

ALSO BY MILLY TAIDEN

Find out more about Milly Taiden here:

Email: millytaiden@gmail.com

Website: http://www.millytaiden.com

Facebook: http://www.facebook.com/millytaidenpage

Twitter: https://www.twitter.com/millytaiden

If you liked this story, you might also enjoy the following by Milly Taiden:

The Crystal Kingdom

Fae King *Book One*

Elf King *Book Two*

Dark King *Book Three*

Fire King *Book Four*

The Crystal Kingdom: New Worlds

Savage King *Book Five*

Warrior King *Book Six*

Guardian King *Book Seven*

Casters & Claws

Spellbound in Salem *Book One*

Seduced in Salem *Book Two*

Spellstruck in Salem *Book Three*

Surrendered in Salem *Book Four*

Alpha Geek

Alpha Geek: *Knox*

Alpha Geek: *Zeke*

Alpha Geek: *Gray*

Alpha Geek: *Brent*

Alpha Geek: *Bennett*

Alpha Geek: *Shaw*

Nightflame Dragons

Dragons' Jewel *Book One*

Dragons' Savior *Book Two*

Dragons' Bounty *Book Three*

Dragon's Prize *Book Four*

Wintervale Packs

Their Rising Sun *Book One*

Their Perfect Storm *Book Two*

Their Wild Sea *Book Three*

Their Controlled Chaos *Book Four*

A.L.F.A Series

Elemental Mating *Book One*

Mating Needs *Book Two*

Dangerous Mating *Book Three*

Fearless Mating *Book Four*

Savage Shifters

Savage Bite *Book One*

Savage Kiss *Book Two*

Savage Hunger *Book Three*

Savage Caress *Book Four*

Paranormal Dating Agency

Twice the Growl *Book One*

Geek Bearing Gifts *Book Two*

The Purrfect Match *Book Three*

Curves 'Em Right *Book Four*

Tall, Dark and Panther *Book Five*

The Alion King *Book Six*

There's Snow Escape *Book Seven*

Scaling Her Dragon *Book Eight*

In the Roar *Book Nine*

Scrooge Me Hard *Short One*

Bearfoot and Pregnant *Book Ten*

All Kitten Aside *Book Eleven*

Oh My Roared *Book Twelve*

Piece of Tail *Book Thirteen*

Kiss My Asteroid *Book Fourteen*

Scrooge Me Again *Short Two*

Born with a Silver Moon *Book Fifteen*

Also, check out the **Paranormal Dating Agency World on Amazon**

Or visit http://mtworldspress.com

ALSO BY MILLY TAIDEN

Sassy Mates / Sassy Ever After Series

Scent of a Mate *Book 1*

A Mate's Bite *Book 2*

Unexpectedly Mated *Book 3*

A Sassy Wedding *Short 3.7*

The Mate Challenge *Book 4*

Sassy in Diapers *Short 4.3*

Fighting for Her Mate *Book 5*

A Fang in the Sass *Book 6*

Also, check out the **Sassy Ever After World on Amazon or visit http://mtworldspress.com**

The Alien Warrior's Woman *Book One*

The Alien's Rebel *Book Two*

ALSO BY MILLY TAIDEN

Night and Day Ink

Bitten by Night *Book One*

Seduced by Days *Book Two*

Mated by Night *Book Three*

Taken by Night *Book Four*

Dragon Baby *Book Five*

Shifters Undercover

Bearly in Control *Book One*

Fur Fox's Sake *Book Two*

Black Meadow Pack

Sharp Change *Black Meadows Pack Book One*

Caged Heat *Black Meadows Pack Book Two*

Other Works

The Hunt

Wynters Captive

Every Witch Way

Hex and Sex Set

Alpha Owned

Match Made in Hell

Wolf Fever

ALSO BY MILLY TAIDEN

Contemporary Works

Mr. Buff

Stranded Temptation

Lucky Chase

Their Second Chance

Club Duo Boxed Set

A Hero's Pride

A Hero Scarred

A Hero for Sale

Wounded Soldiers Set

If you enjoyed the book, please consider leaving a review, even if it's only a line or two; it would make all the difference and would be very much appreciated.

Thank you!

Printed in Great Britain
by Amazon